THE MURDER TRIANGLE

The murder triangle links murderer, victim and detective. Three people are brought together by the death of one of them. The intimate relationships they share lead to further tragedies. For Detective Sergeant Jack Bull, newly recruited into the Serious Incident Unit, the murder triangle is a familiar part of his working life. What no amount of training or experience has prepared him for is participation in a triangle in which he has two of the three roles . . .

LAWRENCE WILLIAMS

THE MURDER TRIANGLE

Complete and Unabridged

LINFORD
Leicester

First published in Great Britain in 1982 by
Robert Hale Limited, London

First Linford Edition
published 2003
by arrangement with
Robert Hale Limited, London

British Library CIP Data

Williams, Lawrence, *1915 –*
    The murder triangle.—Large print ed.—
Linford mystery library
1. Detective and mystery stories
2. Large type books
I. Title
823.9'14 [F]

ISBN 0–7089–4970–3

Published by
F. A. Thorpe (Publishing)
Anstey, Leicestershire

Set by Words & Graphics Ltd.
Anstey, Leicestershire
Printed and bound in Great Britain by
T. J. International Ltd., Padstow, Cornwall

This book is printed on acid-free paper

For Amanda with congratulations

'A plot, or Tragedy, should arise from the gradual closing in of a situation that comes of ordinary human passions . . . '

Thomas Hardy.
(Note in his diary, April 1878.)

'On the distorted face of the Gorgon we see something like an attack of acute schizophrenia. (She foundered in the ocean of the subconscious as symbolized by her love affair with Poseidon.) The hissing hair symbolizes a short circuit, a discharge of electricity — ideas which have overwhelmed her mind.'

Lawrence Durrell.
(*The Greek Islands*, Faber, 1978)

The extract from *The Greek Islands* by Lawrence Durrell is reprinted by permission of Faber and Faber Publishers.

Part One

Tragedy

1

'Come in!'

Not having my crystal ball with me I went in. The snapping of the door-catch separated me from gunfire, screaming tyres and pounding feet.

'Well done, Bull!' Having experienced no difficulty in shutting the door, I raised my eyebrows. 'Well done,' repeated Frimmer, holding out his hand. I submerged my hand in his fist. 'Very few men come through that door at the end of our training programmes. Most go away via the tradesmen's entrance. Eh, Stone?' His companion stepped forward and silently offered me his only hand. Clumsily, I shook it.

Frimmer and Stone looked down at me. I looked up at them. My new suit did not please: reminder of private means. As for Frimmer's jumble-sale costume, I had seen that too many times not to recognise the darns, button spaces, cigar burns: a map of indifference. The close-cropped head rising out of that suit was an anachronism: Bismarck as pauper. I shuffled my feet a bit and glanced at Stone. He was neat enough, but it was always the steel claw that one saw. He stared at me, his long-nosed face as smooth and unruffled as ever. He and Frimmer were the perfect pair to create alarm in a third party.

Feeling distinctly third party I let them manœuvre me onto a wooden chair facing Stone across a desk littered with papers. Frimmer sat on the same side of the desk as me, in a deep leather armchair behind my right shoulder. He rammed his half-finished cigar between his teeth. As he disappeared behind smoke I twisted round to face Stone. They had me at a physical disadvantage as well.

'Welcome to H.Q., the Serious Incident Unit,' barked Frimmer. 'The wallpaper's Stone's work.'

All the walls of the windowless room were covered with graphs and charts. Illumination by spotlights suspended from the ceiling gave the display an air of seedy glamour, as if someone had not quite succeeded in creating a film set of an Operations Room. (Hard to believe that overhead, beyond the air-conditioning grilles, the countryside was edging into spring.) There were only two doors; one by which I had entered and one I knew better than to ask about.

'Shame you needed space for doors,' I said. Frimmer reappeared through the smoke, looked at me, said nothing. Neither of us had mellowed since our last meeting.

'The charts remind us of where we've got to,' said Stone, peaceably.

'And where we're going,' growled Frimmer.

My neck was beginning to hurt. I moved my chair back six inches.

'Talking of the future,' said Frimmer, 'even more congratulations. Not only have you completed our course, I can also confirm you in what was previously your acting rank.' The old devil wasn't pleased at all. I had become a bigger item in his budget.

'Thank you very much, sir.' I moved

5

my chair even further back.

'No trouble from your burns?' asked Frimmer, sharply. He did not like fidgets.

'No, sir. Not a twinge.'

'But the grafts show?'

'Yes, sir.'

'Pity. Means you're easily identified.' Not only was he now obliged to pay me more in my rank of Detective Sergeant, he was also getting damaged goods for his money.

'Obvious only when naked, sir.'

'You and your women,' said Frimmer, obliquely and not good-humouredly. There was a long silence while we thought about women in my past, and the various ways they had scarred me.

'We have an interesting first case for you,' said Stone, abruptly. 'It also involves women.'

'I think you'd better start at the beginning, Stone,' said Frimmer. 'It'll give Bull an idea how S.I.U. has been working.'

'Yes, sir,' said Stone, resting his left hand on the papers on his desk. The steel claw was buried in his pocket. 'We've made a statistical analysis of what's been happening to ex-convicts. We've identified a group of thirty men who have died in the last four years and for whom all the inquest verdicts were misadventure or accidental death. None of them was involved in anything criminal when he died. The next coincidence was that for all of them their last conviction had been for assault on a woman, either rape or G.B.H.' He paused. I said nothing, but he knew I was hooked.

'Even more extraordinary,' said Stone, 'is that for nineteen of the thirty deaths there were no witnesses. That's a higher proportion than that of road accidents having no witnesses. We decided to stay with those nineteen — for the moment. They include five drownings, three single vehicle road crashes at isolated danger spots, four heart failures, seven domestic accidents involving fires, electrocutions etc.

'I don't know how you react to all this, but I'm just about prepared to believe the seven various domestic accidents, particularly in view of the low intelligence and/or mental derangement of some victims. But five drownings — never! Can you think of any criminal group in which twenty-five per cent of the members get drowned in four years? Just to check I ran a programme on all British merchant seamen with criminal records. The percentage drowned over four years was nought point seven per cent. The next question was obvious.'

'Who was doing it?' I suggested.

'Not for us,' said Stone. 'That question is for the man in the field. No, we asked, 'Why? Why *those* nineteen?' We came up with a possible answer almost at once.' Stone paused dramatically. Even Frimmer, who knew the answer, was staring at him.

'All nineteen men had received sentences leading to complaints about leniency. In some of the rape cases defence lawyers had thrown doubt on the veracity and morality of the victims to the extent that a relatively light sentence had been awarded. In other cases juries had difficulty in reaching a verdict, and this also affected sentencing. Don't tell me it shouldn't! We all know it shouldn't!

'By this time we were getting a bit punch-drunk. The odds that all these coincidences might come together *coincidentally* are about the same as you winning half a million on the football pools. We were almost disappointed to discover that there is no statistically significant connection between prison discharge dates and death dates. They were not killed — er, did not die I suppose I should still say — in the order in which they were released. Nor in any other significant order. The theory of crazy warders knocking them off as they were released does not fit. Neither is there any kind of link with the prisons in which they were held. For example, all the drowned men did not come from Parkhurst.

'You know from my lectures during the training course that this type of analysis is suspect. But you will also appreciate my point about the odds against getting such results.'

We sat and appreciated the point. While we did so Frimmer's cigar died. He did not light another. My interview was nearly over.

'A major complication,' said Stone, 'is that if the link between death and the rape is a significant link then we are dealing with a long time-span. The last man to die was discharged three years ago after serving four years for rape. We are proposing links between deaths and crimes committed in different decades. Are you with me?'

'Yes, sir.' I was beginning to feel sorry for myself. I had been looking forward to something immediate which demanded flair not historical research. And what had all my retraining been in aid of? Frimmer was getting ready to tell me.

'Right, Bull,' he said. 'You'll be working with an old friend of yours: Detective Inspector Susan Green. She'll be wet-nurse and guide.'

'Not Detective Sergeant Susie — '

'The same, promoted,' said Frimmer, smugly. 'The one who rescued you from the fire.'

'I report to her, do I?'

'You both report to me,' said Frimmer,

sharply. 'You can now go away and read nineteen fat files. D.I. Green's already read 'em. After you've caught up with her, you and I'll meet again.'

'How urgent, sir, after all these years?'

'Immediate, you sarky bugger. I want you out on the street earning the ridiculous salary I now have to pay you.'

'If our sums are right you'll earn it,' said Stone, grimly. 'Someone who's disposed of at least nineteen victims won't hesitate at number twenty.'

2

Rain and traffic were solid. I squinted at myself in the driving-mirror: J. Bull, Claims Negotiator, Department of Health and Social Security. Under the greasy trilby was bleached hair; below that plain lens spectacles with National Health wire frames; lower still a blonde moustache. I no more liked me than I liked the job. Only a man as warped as Frimmer could have come up with so heartless a scheme: pretending to people already deeply distressed that some form of help might be available for them. He would justify this cruel hoax by pointing to the large number of deaths in suspicious circumstances. The ends and means argument. I suppose that argument partly explained my willingness to be involved. But I needed to believe it was something more than just a case of obeying orders. The lights changed. The traffic moved a few feet and stopped.

I was driving toward the eighth of my nine interviews. For some reason, possibly malice, Frimmer had given me first choice from the nineteen and allocated the remainder to Susan Green. My lady D.I. had not batted a lovely eyelid. Her manner toward me was entirely professional. Not only was I not going to enjoy her luscious body now, I was also forgiven for rejecting it in the past. Initially, this drove me wild, not with frustrated lust, but because there is something peculiarly irritating about an injured party being the magnanimous one. Now, knowing her experience was the same as mine, I felt sympathy for her. Depression caused by the weather, the traffic, the irritations of disguise, was nothing compared with the effects of the tragedies we had begun to probe. Like most of my colleagues I have strong views on capital punishment for murder. Now I have views on extending it.

My first interview had been with a victim of grievous bodily harm. The G.B.H. was so bad the young woman, Miss Wilkinson, was permanently facially

13

disfigured and confined to a wheel-chair. Yet her mother had almost gloatingly assured me all would be well. At least her daughter had not been raped. Because the man had not touched her daughter between the legs there would be nothing to worry about. I had looked into the victim's crooked face and she had looked at me. My merely male bewilderment seemed to be shared. Was rape really so horrible if afterward there was still walking, dancing, running; still possibilities of love?

She might have lost her bewilderment had she come to my second interview and met John Harmon, ex-husband of a rape victim. He had never been able to clear his mind of innuendoes uttered in court by defence counsel. His unfortunate wife had been driven away by his suspicions that she must have encouraged her attacker. Nine years had passed, the divorce was six years old, yet still he had turned on me and cried out that she must have done something to make the man think she was willing. I wasted no words of sympathy on him. Had it been possible

I might have expressed some to his ex-wife, but she had killed herself four years ago. It was that second interview that had begun the process of changing my bewilderment to anger. Now, approaching my eighth interview, I had come to understand that rape can be a kind of death. The deepest agony seems to be in the raping of the spirit that accompanies the act. It is indescribable. More than one spirit is violated: woman, husband, children, parents, friends. It is not so much the grossness of the act itself that destroys but rather the revulsions and hypocrisies that grow out of it. I realise I am groping for words partly because I am not a woman, partly because words fail. Now, when I hear the foolish words of doddering old judges (male) and smart young defence counsel (male) I wish they had accompanied me to my interviews.

Somewhere, someone gave the South London traffic an enema. I risked a quick glance at the A to Z on the seat beside me, swung the battered Ford left at the lights. I found my way to Ridout

15

Crescent, parked a few yards from Number 22. I listened to the rain drumming on the roof of the car. Unfortunately, Frimmer has ideas both fixed and accurate about dress for social workers. As a result I was wearing sandals and a leaky old raincoat. Cursing Frimmer, I grabbed my briefcase (Me with a briefcase!) and splashed to Number 22. The door was opened by a large negro.

'Mr Bull,' I said. 'Department of Health and Social Security. Brigadier French is expecting me.'

'He was, mister. But you're awful late.'

'Er — yes. Sorry. Traffic was bad.'

'You wait there. I'll see if you can be seen.'

Quick footwork thwarted his attempt to shut me out in the rain. I ignored his angry stare.

'Stay on that mat, mister. Just you dry off a bit before you get on my floors.' He went away, all two hundred pounds of him, mostly muscle.

I looked round the tiny, panelled hall at mementoes of the Brigadier's successful career: photographs, citations, animal heads, guns. None of the nineteen had been shot. Had he used his retirement to learn new ways of killing?

When the negro returned he crossly accepted my grubby raincoat and hat, sneered at my sweat-shirt and jeans, ordered me to wipe my sandals yet again and then follow him to the study.

'That Mr Bull,' he muttered, and shut me in with Brigadier French.

The room was only a small suburban sitting-room, but the book-lined walls justified the title of study. The atmosphere was oppressive partly because of the roaring fire.

'Good day, Mr Bull,' said the Brigadier. He did not offer to shake hands but stood and looked at me across the carpet. A small, slim, white-haired man: taut as a stressed steel wire.

'You seem very wet,' he said, abruptly. 'Sit there by the fire. Put your briefcase in the hearth.' A pause. 'Understand the traffic's bad.'

'Yes, sir. Sorry I'm late.' Steam was rising from my socks.

17

'Think you need a drink, Bull. Best defence against the damp.'

'Er — yes — thank you, sir.' To hell with rôle. For all he knew Bull was a dypso.

'Whisky, I think.' He opened the cabinet under the window. The room was so small I could read the labels from where I sat. His hand hovered over two bottles. Then he made up his mind. It's not everyone who offers his best whisky to a stranger. Perhaps he was apologising for his curtness.

Why I had selected Brigadier French or, more correctly, his daughter, Isobel, as one of my interviewees I was not sure. Something in the files had stirred a response in me. But, just as a photograph never quite conveys movement, so words in a file never fully portray the living subject. There would be a mismatch between the man and the thousands of words I had read about him. As I sipped the excellent whisky I acknowledged two facts not in the Brigadier's file. He had a generous heart and he was getting ready to lie to me. What I did not know was whether he would lie because everyone lies about rape or because he had revenged nineteen different women by skilfully murdering their attackers. The idea was ridiculous, but I was being paid to consider it. I try to give value.

'Very surprised to receive your letter,' he said, sitting to attention in his armchair on the other side of the fireplace. 'Not a matter I wish to discuss. Especially as Isobel wants no more to do with it.' For a moment something like firelight showed in his eyes.

'We understand that point of view, sir. We move very tactfully in these circumstances.'

'Precisely what is it you want, Mr — er — '

'Bull, sir.' He knew my name well enough. How many times had he read my letter before agreeing to meet me? 'Neither I nor the Department *want* anything, sir. It is simply that new legislation empowers us to offer help to the victims of criminal assaults in those cases where considerable medical treatment was required.'

'Bit late, isn't it? Isobel was attacked eight years ago.'

'It must seem like that, sir. But the legislation is new. In addition, we are also empowered to seek redress, on her behalf, from your daughter's — er — assailant.'

'Much good may that do.'

'Why do you say that, sir?'

'Can you imagine a rat like that having any assets? And can you imagine for one moment that I or Isobel would accept money obtained from him?'

I sipped my drink. Was he just angry or covering his negotiation of the first hurdle? He had not revealed he knew the man was dead. But the language was not quite right. ' 'Can you imagine a rat like that — ' ' A dissonance there. Try again.

'I understand your feelings, sir, but — '

'But nothing! You can have no idea of my feelings. No idea!'

'No, sir. But I have been doing this job for some time and have met a number of women who have suffered the same kind of experience as your daughter.'

He avoided my eyes, gazed into the fire

for several seconds. Then he spoke sadly, not aggressively.

'How can you bear your job?'

'Because I can offer help to other people.'

'They accept — the help I mean?'

'Sometimes. For some people the help is in talking about an experience they are generally unable or afraid to talk about. For others, a minority, the practical help is important.'

'You offer money?'

'Tactfully, sir, tactfully. Sometimes the help is to put them in touch with a particular facility within the Health Service.' (If only you could hear me, Mr Frimmer!)

'Psychiatrists you mean?'

'Maybe. In some cases the help is to cope with physical disabilities.'

'Cases? God! We're a case, are we? And what do you mean by physical disabilities?'

'Well, sir, some victims of rape are left physically crippled and — '

'Crippled physically *as well* is what you mean!'

21

'Er — maybe, sir.'

'Mr Bull, you must excuse me. I get very angry.' He paused, not looking at me. 'All this concern, but they let rapists off.'

'I'm not a lawyer, sir.'

'You don't have to be, do you?'

'Well, I don't know the legal ins and outs.' Keep prodding.

'Three years for rape doesn't require you to be a lawyer, Mr Bull. And he got a year off for good behaviour! How can that be a proper punishment?'

'I suppose that depends — ' But he was wasn't going to let me talk about circumstances. That might imply Isobel had contributed to her own fate.

'Depends! Depends! D'you think I don't *know* what my daughter has suffered? Execution would've been too good for the man!'

'Execution, sir?'

'Yes. If he ever comes near me I'll certainly kill him.'

'Please, sir, please. Interviewing you and your daughter will not lead to that happening, I assure you.'

'And I assure you, Mr Bull, you'll not interview my daughter.'

'She is of age, sir,' I said, gently.

'Then why interview me? Anyway, she's away.'

'I interview a relative first, sir, because we have learnt from experience that this is sometimes a tactful way to begin.' No reply. I stood up, pushed my spectacles back against the top of my nose. Mr Bull of D.H.S.S. was feeling embarrassed and affronted. 'I do assure you, sir, that — '

'Sit down, man! You must excuse me. Living with Isobel every day — '

'I think I understand, sir.' I walked slowly, damply, to the window. 'She's down in Bournemouth is she, sir?'

'Bournemouth?'

'You said she was away and you have a second home there, sir. Our records show — '

'Your records are out of date. I sold that property years ago.'

'Oh, did you, sir?' And did he know he had sold it only a few weeks before his daughter's attacker was released? And did he know the rapist had elderly parents in

Bournemouth, had no other home to return to? I hunched my shoulders, peered out at the garden. The link was more tenuous than the spiders' webs glistening in the rain.

As for the lie about Isobel being away — that need not be significant; merely a father being protective. But I knew from surveillance reports that his daughter no longer ventured further than the local shops and park, and always with her mother.

On the desk to my right was a photograph of a young woman. She was quite unlike the woman in our file photographs. I knew Isobel was an only child.

'You have another daughter, sir?'

'No. That's Isobel, my Isobel. Taken a long time ago. Before.'

'When may I call and see her?'

'I'm very opposed to this idea, you know.' He looked quickly at his watch.

'Yes, sir. All I can say is your daughter is entitled to the same rights, the same help as anyone else if she wants it. That decision is legally and morally hers. It is also a matter on which she can take advice from you or anyone else she trusts.'

'I will discuss the matter with her. Now if you will excuse me.' Brigadier French looked at his watch again. My late arrival was leading to late departure, and he was expecting his wife and daughter back any minute. I wondered how he had persuaded them to go out on such a foul morning. Very slowly I walked to my seat, picked up my glass and finished the whisky.

'You understand, sir, your daughter has to make the decision?'

'Yes, yes.'

'Perhaps you can suggest a day and time when I can call again?'

'I'll telephone your office. I've got the number on your letter. Now please — '

'Thank you for the drink, sir.' I picked up my briefcase. 'I have a coat and hat.'

'Oh, yes. I'll get Atkins to find them.' He almost ran from the room.

Movement in the garden caught my attention. Someone was opening the gate in the high wall. I stepped close to the window so the light fell directly on my face. Two women, carrying shopping bags, umbrellas clashing, entered the garden and walked along the path toward me. Even though I knew what to expect I still caught my breath. Now I saw the burdens of the victim literally personified in the flesh.

Isobel French had more than doubled her body weight since the rape. She was now safe from every man behind a self-containing wall of fat. Her shapeless clothes held her flesh against her skeleton, but where that support was missing folds of flesh hung loose. A great muffler of chins dragged her head down at an unnatural angle and the original lines of her face were lost in pallid fat. Impossible that this gross body contained the same spirit that had lived in the smiling girl in the desk photograph. Or was it? I felt sick.

There was no possibility that Isobel French had revenged herself. It was only the wiry strength of the sparrowlike woman she leaned on that enabled her to move out of the house. Mrs French looked through the window at me. Fear distorted her face. Hurriedly, she steered her enormous child away from the window. Isobel French did not even see me. Perhaps she was no longer permitted to see, not even after eight years. Some victims' mothers rejoice in their child's captivity. Isobel was twenty-nine years old. I turned from the window.

Atkins was standing behind me. He had forgotten he was carrying my hat and coat. Dumbly, I held out my hands for them. I had not previously seen a Negro turn pale.

3

'We had little warning of your coming, Mr Bull,' said Mrs Athelsteyn-Crump, in a messiah-rebuking voice.

'The Department did write,' I said, somewhat sulky.

'Writing to Miss Grey did not *automatically* ensure that I knew of your visit.' I said nothing. 'You left your car in the car park, I trust, not in the lane?'

'Yes.'

'Then let us walk down the drive together. Thank you, Arthur.'

Arthur, the lodgekeeper nodded at her and, as she turned away, he grinned at me, raised his eyes heavenward.

He swung the great wooden gates together behind us. Odd effect: we were imprisoned in open country. Ahead, the tree-lined drive was noisy in the gale. In the distance stood a great house; the destination I did not much want to reach. Within waited my final sad interview, likely to differ from the other eight only in the greater intensity of misery. My only interview in an institution.

'There are our friends' vegetable gardens,' said Mrs Athelsteyn-Crump, beating back the gale with her formidable handbag. 'Gardening is *such* a blessing for them, so therapeutic, you know.' I didn't, but halted to avoid the swinging handbag and ample backside of my guide. 'Of course, West House is *not* a mental hospital, more a retreat, so people staying here do not have to have constant supervision. Although voluntary helpers like myself donate the seeds and tools, our friends are encouraged to cultivate their plots quite independently.'

'No sign of friends today,' I said, unwisely.

'Then we'll take a quick look. I'm sure you'll be interested.'

She led me off the drive and up into the allotments. Gardening I hate and avoid. It looked as if most inmates — er, friends — shared my feelings. Only the plot sizes and shapes were regular; everything else was muddle and neglect.

Most plots had reverted to a wildscape. The few that were cultivated, for some reason those at the top of the slope, were dingy with old cabbages and a shaggy green plant I could not identify.

'Good cabbages,' I said.

'I suppose so,' said my guide. 'I think it a pity so many of our friends cannot plant out in straight rows.' The vegetables quivered indignantly in the wind.

'You prefer the plot over there?' I asked, like a cemetery keeper.

'Ah, yes. That is the work of our friend, Mr Johnson.' She smiled fondly. I looked at the exceptional patch where nothing moved in the wind and decided Mr Johnson was a nutter. (But of course he was!) 'And there is Mr Johnson. I'll introduce you to him.' She pointed at a faded mackintosh lying at the far end of the plot. As we walked up the side path the mackintosh rose out of the ground as a small, grey grief-smitten man holding a vicious-looking penknife in his right hand and some lengths of string in his left. I could not guess his age. 'Hello, Mr Johnson,' bawled Mrs Athelsteyn-Crump.

'Watcha want and look where you're walking, Mrs Crumpet,' said Mr Johnson, curtly.

'I thought you might like to meet our new visitor. This is Mr Bull who has come to see your friend, Miss Grey. He is interested in gardening, I believe.'

'Bet he ain't,' said Mr Johnson. 'And mind your great feet,' he added, glaring at me. I looked down at the theodolite balanced on wedged bricks. He must have been lying down squinting through it as we approached. 'Jest got it set level. That third cabbage along's been giving me trouble.'

The cabbage indicated had some of its outer leaves on the south side pulled slightly out of line, presumably by its natural desire to reach toward the sun. I looked across the plot. It was as worrying from this side as from the other. No naturalness was permitted in cabbages. Each row was horrifyingly straight, and each member of each row had been heavily staked to prevent it inclining from the vertical. Every cabbage had its outer leaves tied in, except for the one troublemaking plant at which Mr Johnson's theodolite was aimed. I was looking at a physical representation of madness: an endeavour pushed beyond reason. I shivered.

'Move on, woman!' snapped Mr Johnson. 'Too cold to hang about chatting. I've work to finish.'

'Oh — yes,' said Mrs Athelsteyn-Crump, blushing slightly.

I turned to follow her, was detained by Mr Johnson seizing my arm in a spiteful grip.

'Careful of her, youngster. Not safe with us men. With a name like Crumpet. Why d'you think she calls us all friends?'

'Er — thanks,' I said, backing away.

'Now that Miss Grey — '

I stopped shuffling my feet.

'What about her, Mr Johnson?'

'A *real* lady she is, not newview rich like this cow. Ever so kind to me. Not surprised she don't live here full time. She's too good to be shut up with the rest of us.'

'Kind to you?'

'Brings me things when she comes.

Cooks special meals for me. Wonderful person, especially when you realise how she's suffered.' He rubbed his face with the palms of his hands. 'But she's here to be away from your sort. You do her any harm and I won't be the only one after your guts!'

I attempted to soothe him, but Mrs Athelsteyn-Crump intervened.

'Come away,' she called up the slope toward me. 'We must not get Mr Johnson excited.'

'Piss off!' shrieked Mr Johnson, so we did. But as I hurried after my guide I looked back over my shoulder. Mr Johnson mouthed one word at me and the soft sound of it drifted downslope like the wind sighing in the trees.

'Mr Johnson is a little strange at times,' said Mrs Athelsteyn-Crump, as I caught up with her on the drive. 'But we must be charitable, he's been here a long time.'

I wondered how charitable she would be if she had heard everything he had said.

As we entered the house she pointed at a row of chairs in the hall. 'Wait here, please. I'll let Miss Grey know you've arrived.' Then she began to puff her way up the stairs.

I sat down and discovered my chair faced a wall-mirror. I had accepted my facial disguise by this time. It was the costume that disgusted. The worn, pale grey ill-cut suit was the least offensive part of it. I averted my gaze from the Fair Isle pullover only to find I was looking at the cerise tie worn with the blue and white striped shirt. Disaster if I met my tailor: turn him into an inmate of West House.

'Our friend, Miss Grey, will be pleased to receive you, Mr Bull,' announced Mrs Athelsteyn-Crump, rolling to a stop at the foot of the stairs. 'Her sitting-room is Room 14, upstairs and along the corridor. Just knock on the door. I shall remain here. It is where I usually sit until tea-time. In case I am needed, you know.' She opened her capacious handbag and pulled out knitting. She was working on a Fair Isle pullover. Hated her knitting, envied her calm.

On the first floor landing was another

full length mirror. A young man with snow-white hair talked softly to his reflection. I edged past. The door of Room 14 stood wide open. There was nothing institutional about the interior. It was attractively furnished with comfortable armchairs standing on a dark brown carpet. The flower-print curtains matched the wallpaper, a vase of daffodils stood on the small occasional table, and a modern gas fire hissed gently in the far wall. A doorway led off to a small pink bedroom. A feminine well-loved home. Home? Feeling foolish and shabby in my disguise I hesitated, hesitated also for less superficial reasons. I tapped on the open door.

'Come in, Mr Bull.' She spoke from behind the door. I peered round the edge of it as she rose from the little writing-desk and held out her hand. 'How do you do?'

'Miss Grey, Miss Madelaine Grey?'

'Yes.'

Awkwardly, we stood facing each other. She was tall, elegant in a high-necked grey wool dress and pearls. Not beautiful but having that aristocratic cool style: fine skin, broad forehead, straight nose, brown hair lightly waved and back from her face; her grey eyes wide behind those very large fashion spectacles that suit few women. They suited her. Difficult to accept she was thirty-five.

'We could sit down by the fire,' she drawled, walking across the room. She was lean, long-thighed, broad-shouldered. Slightly unexpected that she was not wearing a bra.

I sat in the chair she indicated, she on the opposite side of the fire with the windows behind her. Her face was almost lost to me against the light. In her spectacles I saw only myself. I looked down at the exceptionally beautiful, long-fingered hands clasped in her lap. They were still. Her silence implied inward peace; mine implied disgust. I wanted to reject the knowledge I possessed, especially those coldly eloquent medical reports on the state of her body after the rape. But then I had *chosen* her as one of my interviewees. Not sure why. Champion swimmer, and we were dealing with drownings; mentally unstable, and we suspected mass murder; extraordinarily calm in court despite hostile cross-examination, and we were looking for someone extraordinary. Detectives live in a world of no certain thing. Her hands moved abruptly. I had been staring. She smoothed her skirt.

'Kind of you to see me, Miss Grey. You understood my letter?'

'Yes, Mr Bull. I received it just before I left home to come here.'

'I see.'

'I think not!' This was said with such ferocity I jumped. She looked coldly at me. 'There is not much about my situation you are likely to see — as you put it.' This sudden excursion into rage was alarming. I wondered how to fetch a nurse.

'You understand that I am a short-stay voluntary patient?' Her voice was calm again.

'Er — yes.'

'Only a private nursing home like this can cope with my needs. I am able to come here when things get bad. Otherwise I lead a normal life.'

The rueful note in her voice, slight shrugging of the shoulders were more expressive than medical reports. Every day this apparently self-possessed woman had to struggle for possession of her own mind. And now she was here because she had been losing the struggle.

'I'm sorry you've had to come back here, Miss Grey. I wish we could have met in your home.'

'Thank you, Mr Bull. But I've learnt to love this place not only because of what it does but also because of what it is. It is a place of renewal as well as retreat.' She looked down at her feet, then directly into my face. 'I expect to be here every year about this time. February to May is the suicide season.' She spoke so calmly I almost believed I misheard. We were silent for some time.

'I've come to see if my department can help you.' The words were abrupt, dragged out of me. 'We are now empowered to help out financially and in other ways.' I was getting worse with each interview.

'I understand what you are trying to

38

say.' Her hands came together again in her lap. 'But I have a good job, considerate colleagues, a nice flat — and this place when I need it.'

'Yes, I see. But that does not disqualify you from receiving help from us directly and from your attacker indirectly.'

'My attacker?' She began rubbing her hands together and rocking gently from side to side.

'Why shouldn't he be made to assist you?'

'Do you really think? — Doesn't matter. Waste of time.' She crouched as if preparing to spring on me.

'What do you mean?'

'He's dead. Died two years ago.'

'I didn't realise you knew that. I'm sure you don't want to talk about it.' Bumbling Bull still needling. Would she pick up my mistake?

'Mr Bull, I don't *mind*. I knew him of course before the attack. He was a local boy; same Youth Club, same Tennis Club as myself. Always very quiet and withdrawn. The fact we knew each other and he was the retiring one was used against me in court.' She drew a deep breath. 'It was in the local paper — that he died, I mean. He was — was drowned. In a lake in a park near his home, near my former home. I was staying here when it happened, but a friend sent me a copy of the local paper.'

'You were here?'

'Yes. The news didn't help me, you know.'

'You thought he'd already paid his debt?'

'Paid?' Her voice hardened. 'Men like that *never* pay, never enough. And they want to do it again. Rapists are always, always on the lookout for the next victim. A few months in prison doesn't change an animal except to make it more animal. I want them all to die, Mr Bull. I hope they all die.' So did I now, but I had to keep the interview moving.

'No, Miss Grey — '

'No? You're either stupid or a fraud, Mr Bull. And what did you mean just now: 'You didn't realise I knew about his death?' How could you suggest he pay if he is dead?' Her eyes glittered. She sprang to her feet, paced up and down. I looked for a bell-push. There wasn't one. 'What do you really want, Mr Bull? Am I just another cog in a piece of research? Are you a sex freak of some kind?'

'Not at all. You know who — '

'Let's try you out.' Carefully, she took off her reading glasses and put them on the shelf over the fire. Then she burst into frenzied action: ripping down the zip of her dress, stepping out of it naked. The string of pearls snapped, flew in every direction, rolling, bouncing. Then she was in my lap, wriggling herself against me, shuddering. Spittle ran down her chin.

'Come on,' she hissed. 'Tell me what you really want or I'll start screaming rape.'

'Please, Miss Grey! Really!'

'Come on, little man. Let's have those spectacles off!'

'Really, I protest! Dress yourself!'

'I'm going to scream.'

'But I'm a respectable man. And you are the one undressed!'

'Blame the woman again, will you? Not your fault. You were led on. As judge you'd give a stupid short sentence. What's the verdict when I scream?'

'They won't believe you this time, either.' Sick with self-disgust I delivered the blow.

Her breath hissed between her clenched teeth. Then, very slowly, she slithered off my lap and onto the floor, round breasts brushing across my thighs, down my legs. She huddled at my feet, clutching my ankles. She neither sobbed nor cried out, but huge tears ran down her face, fell into the crevices of her folded body. I leaned forward, held out both hands. She made no attempt to stand but took my hands childlike against her face, bathed them with her tears. So we sat, silent together and warm before the fire.

Later, when her breathing had quietened, the room was possessed by the hiss of the gas fire, the buffeting of the wind against the windows. Her scent, her nakedness began to fill the space of the room, to fill my senses. I freed one hand, smoothed her hair, touched the line of her eyebrows.

'You are sad for me?' she asked at last.

'And for others like you.'

'Ah.' Gently, she pressed her face against my knee. 'You understand.'

'Not sure I do.'

'To let me sit here so long like this — no fuss. Did you take off my dress?'

'No, you did.'

'And my pearls?'

'You were in a — a rage. You broke them.'

'Please shut your eyes.'

Rather nervously I did so, felt her move away from me, heard the dress rustle.

'You can look now.' She was standing in front of me dressed except for her shoes and the pearls. 'I don't really know what to say, Mr — er — Bull. I'm not even quite sure what happened.'

'Then say nothing about it. Tell me instead about your life here.'

She sat down in the chair opposite me, breathed slowly and deeply. After a long pause she began to talk, to turn a police file into heartrending reality.

Thirty minutes later I went downstairs, leaving her crouching over the cast pearls. I met Mrs Athelsteyn-Crump in the hall.

'I hope your visit went well, Mr Bull. I was beginning to wonder if I should come up.'

'Er — no. Everything was quite all right. I may call again in a few days. I'll telephone first. Thank you for your help.'

I walked quickly along the drive. The wind moaned in the plane trees. On the hillside slope some cabbages stood perfect in their rows. No sign of human life. From up there Mr Johnson had whispered one word, had sent it grinding down the slope as coldly as the glacier that had once scoured it: ' 'Death.' '

4

The telephone rang me out of sleep.
04.15. Wrong number or emergency.
Blundered onto the landing. Mrs Giles,
my landlady, gave a muffled squeak, fell
back into her room, wrappings swirling.
Muttering apologies I crabbed down the
stairs.

'Mr Bull?'

'Speaking.'

'Identify.'

'D.H.S.S. two-nine-three stroke seven.'

'Duty Officer Jim Douglas here. You'll
have to pretend your Auntie's died.
There'll be a car at the door in fifteen
minutes. Got that?'

'Fifteen minutes. Yes.'

'A word to the wise, Jack. Frimmer will
be in the car.'

'Thanks. I'll be ready.'

I climbed the stairs trailing my bowels
behind me. Risking my cover meant
something big. And Frimmer coming!

Mrs Giles clutched at me. I took control of bowels and landlady.

'Sorry you were disturbed, Mrs Giles, but my Aunt Mavis is dying. A car's being sent.' I brushed past her flapping arms and squeaky regrets. Frimmer would give me more trouble than she.

In ten minutes I was ready. I checked the room. There were writing-papers on the table. I stuffed them into a folder, put it under sweaters in the bottom drawer of the wardrobe. Minimise the chance of Mrs Giles discovering I was writing poetry. I had only just found out myself. Perhaps it was a response to bedsit boredom. Perhaps it was something to do with the stress of rôle playing when my feelings were becoming deeply involved. Tush — as they say. Muttering my way down the stairs I was again pawed by Mrs Giles waiting for me in the hall.

'Ever so sorry, Mr Bull. You take this. Seeing as it's a nasty wet morning and so early.' She thrust a vacuum flask into my hands. 'Coffee. No sugar. Just as you like it. Far to go, dear?'

46

'Er — quite a way. That's why the car is coming instead of me driving.'

'Least they could do, this time of night. You keep yourself warm, Mr Bull. You don't want to catch a cold.'

'I will. Thanks very much.'

I hardly had time to shut her front door before, from round the corner, lights struck at wet walls, road nameplate, blind windows of silent houses. Then the headlights were switched off. A black Jaguar, glistening in the rain, parking lights only, came silently into the street, edged over to my side and stopped outside Mrs Giles' gate. Engine turning over, it stood directly under the street lamp. For added reassurance the driver got out of the car and opened the rear door.

'Be brisk, Bull,' called Frimmer from within. 'What's that?' he snapped as I lurched against him.

'Morning, sir. Sorry. Flask of coffee. Mrs Giles is worried about my health.'

'Christ Almighty, Bull! How d'you do it? When they're not dropping 'em for you they're making you meals-on-wheels!'

'Charm, sir.'

'What are you sniggering at?' This to the driver. 'You know the way?'

'Yes, sir.'

'Right then. We'll talk privately. You concentrate on driving — fast!'

Frimmer leaned forward, pressed a button on the back of the driver's seat. A glass screen rose silently between us and the front seats. Despite the gloom I thought I saw the driver's neck change colour. I enjoyed being on the right side of the glass.

'Tell you where we're going presently,' said Frimmer. 'I'd like to bring you up to date first.'

'Yes, sir.'

'I have had two other officers, Wilson and Douglas, recheck the inquest reports. Then we put those with yours and Green's interview reports. As a result I've cut the nineteen cases to thirteen — the most interesting ones. Still included in the reduced list are the people for whom you requested full surveillance. So your intuition'd better be right, Bull. It's costing S.I.U. a bomb.'

I said nothing. Budgeting was his cross not mine.

'Right. French and Harmon first. Nothing from surveillance. Our man lost French two days ago but only for about half an hour in a shopping centre in Croydon. No one we'd care about died in that time.'

'He could've made a phone call?'

'Yes.' Frimmer was curt. 'So could the rest of the population.'

We watched the rain slashing at our headlights, zigzagging obliquely down the side windows. We were almost clear of North London already.

'What I mean is,' he said, creeping suspiciously close to apology, 'if we get stuck with any kind of conspiracy theory we can't handle it. We'd have to seek widespread collaboration from other police services on the basis of very slim evidence.'

'Yes, sir,' I said. What I thought was that he had no intention of sharing any glory either.

'Now, Bull, about Miss Madelaine Grey?'

'Sir.'

'Your report reads like a scene from Raymond Chandler.'

'Maybe. But that's how it was.'

'Don't get stuffy with me, Bull. It's not your truthfulness that worries me but your sex appeal. All right, I accept that you did nothing to encourage her. I also accept that strange sexual behaviour may be characteristic of some of these unfortunate women.'

I stared through the rain at the motorway signs. Soon we could turn off for Watford. I watched for the three hundred yard marker, two hundred, one hundred, goodbye Watford. And he accepts that strange sexual behaviour may be characteristic. How very good of him. I did not want to speak to him, but there was still the job.

'Miss Grey's been checked out, sir?'

'Yes. For eight times of death she was resident in West House, for the other five still on our list she was holidaying in the West Country. On her holidays she hires self-catering places and shares with friends.'

50

'So no clear pattern, sir?'

'No.' We sat and felt sorry about it. 'Absence of pattern insignificant,' said Frimmer, 'especially in the light of a further check you requested.'

'Which one?'

'Security at West House. As you suspected: any reasonably intelligent maniac can get in or out without discovery. But then it's not meant to be a secure establishment; not much more than an ordinary nursing home. There are several places at which fences or walls can easily be scaled. Our man even found a large hole cut in a wire fence. And staff supervision is minimal, expecially at night. Most of the victims died at night.'

'So we're not much further forward there, either?'

'No. Now tell me about this other check you wanted, this Mr Johnson. The first I knew of it was when Stone put a new file on my desk yesterday afternoon. Why d'you want him checked? He's daft as a brush and just as harmless.'

'Maybe so, sir. I could be wasting everybody's time, but he interested me

51

sufficiently to ask for more information.'

'You'll see the file. But tell me why. I don't run S.I.U. just to satisfy the curiosity of my junior staff.'

'No, sir.'

'You sulking, Bull, or is it you can't answer my question? I suppose your intuition's been galloping away with you again.'

'Well — partly. The intuition, I mean. But he's the sort of man who makes me want to question the pattern we've been working on.'

'Widening the field again?'

'Fraid so, sir. Johnson could've been drawn in by proximity. What I mean,' I said, hastily, 'is that he virtually lives with Miss Grey for part of the year and he undoubtedly cares for her. Maybe there's something there: cover-up, collusion. God, I don't *know*!' How could I tell Frimmer about the cabbages, about the whisper of death?

'Take it easy, Bull. I can see raised eyebrows even in this light. You're not under attack. I'm just prodding you on, that's all. One of the few ways I earn my money. And you *could* be right. Why not?

As you know, Miss Grey's parents ditched her in the cruellest possible way. So there she was, desperate for support, meeting this sixty year old Johnson who was desperate for a friend. And both of them barmy.'

'Yes, sir.' I was agreeing with the idea not the language. In front of me the driver adjusted his radio controls. I could distinguish nothing of the message. Frimmer sighed.

'Right, Bull. I'll keep people working on Grey and Johnson. You'll be informed if anything significant comes up.'

'Thank you, sir.'

'Now I suppose I'd better tell you where we're going. But how about some coffee first? Let's see just how much your landlady cares for you. Reckon she hates your guts,' Frimmer said, returning the cup. 'It's paint stripper.'

I took a sip, then poured the dregs back into the flask, screwed down the lid. I had probably manufactured a bomb. Somewhere near my right shoulder, over Suffolk, some other joker was brightening up the sky. I wondered if Frimmer had thought to bring any breakfast.

5

'We're going to a small town in the Midlands,' said Frimmer, vaguely. 'One of the reasons why I don't want *you* widening the scope of our inquiries is that they're already a bloody sight wider than you know!'

'You mean there's something you haven't been telling me, sir?' I was wide awake again.

Frimmer ignored my sarcasm, leaned forward, pressed the partition button. 'Driver, was that last message my confirmation?'

'Yes, sir. Just came through. As you expected.'

'Naturally. Don't take the Wolverhampton road will you?'

'No, sir. I know the route.'

'Hmm,' said Frimmer, pressing the button, watching the glass rise. My ears were laid well back. Frimmer's remarks suggested uneasiness; not characteristic.

'What I haven't told you, Bull, is that in addition to all the follow-up work we're also trying to anticipate our killer — if there is one.' He waited. I said nothing. 'We've been keeping a close watch on a number of rapists recently released from prison. That's why the troops are so thin on the ground. Now is the time for you to know about this.'

'Working for you is like peeling layers off an onion — sir.'

'As long as it don't make you cry.'

'That's not what it does to me.'

'That's all right then, isn't it, Sergeant?' He waited. 'Isn't it?'

'Yes — sir.'

'We've picked out half a dozen villains to keep an eye on,' said Frimmer. 'They qualify on the grounds of disgustingness of their crime, shortness of sentence and amount of publicity given in the Press. Now one of them has given us the slip.'

'You mean he *knew*?' A chance to let out resentment.

'Possibly. Anyhow, we put out an alert and his car's been found up here outside a large park.'

'And in the park there's a lake?'

'Right. When I picked you up the local police were just climbing the railings. Since then they've found him in the lake.'

'That was the last radio message?'

'Yes, Bull. Be there in a few minutes.' He leaned back and closed his eyes. I glanced sideways at his crumpled face. *His* intuition had also been working. We'd started our journey merely because a man had not been seen for a few hours. Merely?

Fifteen minutes later we were wriggling through a hole in the park fence. As we strode across the wet grass, not dodging the young daffodils, we were met by a uniformed Inspector with whom Frimmer began a muttered conversation. I trailed behind them to the lake.

'Joseph Abercrombie, rapist, late of Leicester Gaol, formerly of London.' Frimmer sounded angry.

I looked down at the grounded corpse, one of its legs still trailing in the shallow water of the lakeside. I shivered inside my damp raincoat. Isobel French was more bloated in life than was Abercrombie in death. Our killer was doing a good job. I smiled ruefully, finding myself in agreement with Brigadier French.

'O.K., so we boobed,' snapped Frimmer, misinterpreting the expression on my face. 'We had him covered until about eighteen hours ago in Luton. Then he slipped us. We discovered he had some kind of contact up here so we switched the search. What bloody use it was!'

The Inspector bridled.

'What was he doing in Luton?' I asked.

'Staying with Mum. She told us where he had gone only when we convinced her he might be in danger.'

'And how did he give your tail the slip?'

'Dodgy running in the Arndale shopping centre.'

'So he *did* know he was tailed,' I said.

'It raises questions about the 'job' up here, don't it?'

'Someone told him he was being tailed?'

'Just possible,' said Frimmer.

'Just possible that person knows why as well.'

'Of course.'

'Sir.'

'O.K., O.K. You know we'll look into it. God knows where I find the men.' He smoothed his damp hair. He did not usually discuss his difficulties with underlings. 'You know the other reason why I called you out?'

I looked through the metallic dawn at the assembled policemen, the waiting ambulance and crew, the irritable police surgeon.

'Not short of help here,' I said. I was trying not to lose my temper. I was sick of his manipulative questioning.

'No, but the next tailing job could be yours. So get to know this case inside out — starting now.'

'Can we proceed, sir?' The uniformed Inspector was polite but impatient.

'What?' said Frimmer. 'Oh — yes, Inspector. Make sure I get the medical report as soon as possible. And tell your doc not to assume it was drowning. I'll leave this man here with you.'

'Sir.' The Inspector was not happy. He turned his back on me, walked away and spoke to the doctor.

'Look,' said Frimmer, 'past that clump of willows. Small island with summer-house. Maybe he set out for it in a rowing-boat and never arrived.'

'And the boat?'

'Found drifting. They've tied it up round the corner.'

'Why was he going there this time of year and day?'

'Dunno. Nor does anyone else. He pinched the boat during the night. Not sure how long he's been dead but he looks pretty fresh to me.'

'But there could be one other person who knows apart from Mr Abercrombie,' I said, watching the body being dragged clear of the water.

'And since neither are telling we'll rely on the doctor,' said Frimmer, tartly. 'Go over this site with the locals then report back to Stone. You'll be briefed on our next likely victim. If we don't get a break soon the buggers inside'll be refusing their discharge!'

'This is another for Stone's collection?'

'We're safe in assuming that. Bloody Hell! Another drowned rapist!'

'Mr Stone'll be happy, sir.'

'You push off,' snarled Frimmer. 'I'm for breakfast with the Chief Constable.'

I watched him stalk away. Then I walked to the water's edge. 'Detective Sergeant Bull,' I said to the Inspector.

'Hinchcliffe,' said the Inspector, curtly. 'You with his team?' He jerked his head toward Frimmer climbing through the fence.

'Yes, sir.'

'Tartar?'

'Some say so.'

'What's all the interest?'

'Not the first case like this, sir. Maybe some tie up.'

'Inspector.' It was the doctor who was crouching beside the body now on the stretcher. 'Looks like drowning, but he knocked his head. Contusion behind the right ear. Could be he fell in unconscious.'

'Yes,' said Inspector Hinchcliffe. 'It could happen. He could've stood up to pole himself clear of the bank, slipped and fell in, hitting his head on the gunwale as he fell. You taking him now, Doc?'

'Too right. We don't want any more hanging about.' The doctor gave me an unfriendly look.

'Where's the boat, sir?' I asked.

'This way,' said Hinchcliffe.

The small rowing-boat was tied to a willow tree and guarded by a heavily built uniformed constable about twice my age. There was only one oar in the boat.

'Haven't found it yet, sir,' said the constable, answering my question. 'Probably drifted into the reeds somewhere.'

'Where did he get the boat from in the first place?' I asked.

'Along here, sir,' said the constable, leading the way along the muddy bank. 'This lake's a popular recreation area. The boats are tied up for the start of the season. They'll be back in use in a fortnight.'

We came to a small pier with a shuttered kiosk at the landward end. Nine rowing-boats nudged each other in undulating line abreast. At the end of the line the rope that held them together trailed in the water.

'All he had to do was untie the last boat?' I said.

'Yes, sir,' said the constable.

'Sergeant,' I said, thoughtfully.

'Oh — er, yes, Sergeant,' said the constable.

'The boat was found upside down in the middle of the lake. By the time we got here it had drifted to the side,' said Hinchcliffe.

'Really?' I turned to the constable. 'You righted the boat yourself, did you?'

'Er — yes,' said the constable, looking anxiously at his Inspector.

'You had to, of course,' I said. The constable relaxed. 'Was it easy?'

'Sorry, Sergeant. I don't get — '

'Christ! Was it easy — turning the boat over?'

'Oh — no. You see — the boats are very broad.'

'Right. Now if you got down into one of these boats would it be as hard to reverse the job, overturning it?'

'It might be even harder, Sergeant.'

'Yes,' I said. 'Perhaps easier if standing in the water?'

'You're not suggesting — ' began Hinchcliffe.

'Not yet,' I said. 'All the same it makes you think.'

They stood and thought.

'It seems,' I said, 'that Abercrombie was either barmy, keen on exercise or hoping to meet someone on the island. Can we go there now, sir?'

'Suppose so,' said the Inspector, reluctantly. 'We could use one of these boats here.'

Despite the encumbrance of his waterproof cape, the constable managed to row us across to the tiny landing-stage on the island. I got out first, stood still, then walked forward, instructing the others to follow. I moved very slowly, examining the ground. When we reached the small octagonal summer-house I led them right round it before entering. I sat down on the rough-hewn seat. As if mesmerised, my companions sat facing me. Enjoying suspense, I stared out into the raining dawn while the others stared at me. I turned to the constable.

'Your name?'

'Parks, Sergeant.'

None of us smiled.

'Right, Parks. Tell me what you think of this. You've been out of prison some time, unemployed, no friends in the district where your Mum, your only relative, has moved to. O.K?'

'Er — yes.'

'While staying with Mum someone contacts you with the offer of a job. The job's crooked so you have to be sure you're not followed when you leave. You are told to come to this lake to get instructions. This park is chosen either because it's easy to find or because you know it. Now, when you get here it's still dark. You've been told to row out to the island to meet your contact. How would you feel?'

'Do I know the person who phoned me?' asked Parks, his broad face wrinkled with concentration.

'No idea. Let's assume you do.'

'Then I'm not frightened,' said Parks, thoughtfully.

'What do you need?' I asked.

'A boat,' said Parks, simply.

'What else?'

Parks thought for some time. Hinchcliffe

moved restlessly on the seat, impatient on Parks' behalf.

'I need to know — ' said Parks, nervously, 'to know the other person's already on this island before I'm willing to start the miserable job of rowing across.'

'Good man! And that implies a signal from the island or a message at that kiosk. Now let's assume a light was flashed from this island. Is that feasible?'

'It is,' said Parks.

'Right. Then why are there no footprints here, no sign of anyone being here in the last few days?'

'Because a message was pinned up at the kiosk,' said Hinchcliffe, impatiently.

I stared at him until he flushed with anger. I realised why I was in S.I.U. and he never would be.

'No, sir,' I said at last. 'I didn't leave a message at the kiosk just in case someone else saw it or Abercrombie missed it.'

'Because the job was a big one?' asked Hinchcliffe.

'No. Because I meant to murder the man by drowning him.' My companions glanced at each other. 'You see, our murderer was determined to leave no clue as to his own presence. That's why I can't consider the idea they shared a boat. That's why there was no message — just in case, even on this god-forsaken night — someone else came down here.'

'How was the signal operated from here?' asked Hinchcliffe.

'I think it was flashed from the end of this landing-stage here. Although the outer lake shore is less than fifty yards away that signal would have appeared to come from this summer-house. We're sitting only fifteen feet from the landing-stage.'

'You mean no one landed, the murderer was in another boat?' asked Parks.

'I think not,' I said. 'Another boat might betray the murderer. Say the boats banged against each other, then the damage might be a giveaway. No, he was probably in the water, maybe in a wet suit.'

'Your trouble,' said Hinchcliffe, 'is your imagination is creating a case we cannot possibly solve.'

'Not me, sir. The murderer — and he's an expert by now. And think of the advantage of surprise over Abercrombie.'

We looked out onto the rain-rippled, wind-flecked water, imagining the moment of surprise, of terror. Hands out of black water wrenching on the side of the boat; Abercrombie off-balance, his own weight helping to overturn the boat. Or the victim was stunned first, perhaps with his own oar which he thought he had lost by snagging the bottom of the lake.

'And what do *we* do?' asked Hinchcliffe, irritably.

'Well, sir, there was one thing the murderer could not be certain of concealing, expecially as he could not be sure it would continue to rain.'

'And that was?' asked Hinchcliffe, coldly.

'He had to get into the lake — and out again,' said Parks, excitedly.

'Good lad,' I said. 'For that we'll let you row us back as well.'

6

Five of us sat at a long table in Frimmer's underground bunker, each with a file of papers. Frimmer sat at the head of the table; Stone on his right. I sat next to Stone. Facing me was the other new recruit to S.I.U.: D.S. Jim Douglas. He had not been in my training group, but I had met him several times in our fake D.H.S.S. office. He must be a good man if he got through a similar programme to mine! Pity he was so big, he might be difficult to use in an undercover operation. Lastly, between Douglas and Frimmer sat D.I. Susan Green. I had also met her several times in the office; we'd compared notes on our interviews, even been to the local for drinks together. But how carefully we had avoided reminiscence. Now, under the spotlights of Frimmer's bunker, the sight of her propelled me back into our shared past, our work together on a case in my home town when she had recruited me for S.I.U. She was wearing that familiar silver-blonde wig. I knew that the awful scar round her head would never be concealed by the regrowth of her own hair. And she knew of my scars. So short a time ago that she had knelt over me, her heavy breasts falling into my frantic little hands. To think that she and I had once almost — not the point. The point was that we were again in the same team. I looked round the table again. The obviously extraordinary thing was that only one of us, Jim Douglas, looked anything like the public image of a copper. The other extraordinary thing was that the others were all staring at me.

I had missed something while day-dreaming. The silence pressed. Frimmer had no intention of helping. Stone, thinking me nervous, was more merciful.

'You are happy with Document One, the surveillance list?'

'Oh yes, sir. All my preferences are there: French, Harmon, and then Johnson with Grey as a pair. Peters and Mackie from D.I. Green's interviews also seem

O.K. to me — judging from the files and her interview reports.'

'Right,' said Frimmer. 'Now Document Two. Here is our list of the thirteen victims we've been concentrating on. It was this list plus Document One that I took with me when I went to see the Assistant Commissioner yesterday. Perhaps I should explain for the benefit of our new colleagues that S.I.U. is roughly equivalent to a boil up the backside as far as our A.C. is concerned. He'd like to get rid of us, because we don't fit tidily into the system, but funks the anguish of the operation. It's a case of a good copper turned into an admin. monkey by too many promotions. Unfortunately, one of his admin. duties is approving our budgets. Well, you can imagine what he had to say about these two bits of paper.' Frimmer allowed us a moment to imagine.

'The A.C. expressed himself impressed by the statistics and by the thoroughness with which S.I.U. had followed up the interviews et cetera. However, he felt quite unable to justify the cost of all this unless we could produce something more than clever work with numbers. He was also alarmed that one of our interviewees might actually submit a claim for compensation. I explained that as the only paperwork they had was a letter asking for an interview, and that I could close the London office in less than one hour, the whole thing would be dealt with as a cruel hoax perpetrated by someone unknown. That I was telling the truth upset him even more. However, he was good enough to say that our files would be allowed to remain open while we got on with other more pressing cases.'

We were all on the edges of our seats by this time. Frimmer is a great story-teller. The smirk that was beginning to appear from under his left nostril suggested the punch line was due.

'Lady and gentlemen, I told the A.C two things. Firstly, I told him about Joseph Abercrombie. I pointed out that not only was he our fourteenth rapist victim but also our sixth drowning. I'll not bore you with the next bit of our conversation but move to the second thing I told him, namely, that we had been trying to anticipate our killer by keeping an eye on Abercrombie. The A.C enjoyed underlining our failure there, but he also took the point that we are changing our method of operation.

'The gist of all this is that we will be proceeding exactly as I had planned, with our requirements for surveillance et cetera all included as part of the next stage of the operation. That next stage is represented by Document Three. You will see that we have found another Abercrombie.'

I looked at Document Three. Jake Corelli might be suitable bait: multiple rapist, petty gangster, a record of violence from age twelve.

'Is he out, sir?' asked Green.

'Next week,' said Frimmer.

'Why him, sir?' asked Douglas.

'He fits better than anyone already on the street.'

Something about that answer didn't feel right to me. Maybe it was that feeling that prompted my question. 'Description, sir?'

'Here,' said Frimmer, giving out photographs.

The photographs reached the others before me. They appeared transfixed by what they saw. My copy fluttered face down onto the table in front of me. I turned it over and stripped the final layer from Frimmer's onion. The others stared at me while I struggled with shock. My wariness had never prepared me for anything like this. This. I flicked the photograph with my finger-tips, but it stayed right side up: a photograph of myself.

'Think of the advantages,' said Frimmer, at last.

'I'm thinking that when you recruited me last summer you must already have had this plan in mind,' I said.

'Foresight it's called,' said Frimmer, smugly. 'But we only had this in mind as a remote possibility. At that time we hadn't all the data or — '

'Only a remote possibility?' I said, interrupting Frimmer. 'What a basis for recruiting!'

'Don't make that mistake,' said Stone,

quickly. 'You were selected for our training course very much on merit.'

'We'd've had you anyway,' chuckled Frimmer. 'So don't start bandaging that inflated ego. Now you see the point of my remark when we first met — about your swarthy, gypsy-like appearance. Men who look like policemen aren't always the best buy for S.I.U. And if I had told you then of this possibility think how prejudiced you'd've been.'

'There was also the possibility that we would get a result before this part of our planning became appropriate,' said Stone.

A long silence during which only Stone and Frimmer were prepared to look at me. The trouble was not that my anger was uncontrollable, or that I was deciding the wording of my resignation, but that I was getting interested. And those two foxes knew it. They also knew how the pressure from silent colleagues was working on me. I was on trial in several senses.

'This is what Corelli really looks like,' said Stone, sliding another set of photographs along the table.

'We don't look *that* much alike, do we?'
I asked, defensively.

'No,' said Frimmer, 'but then you don't
have to. Just drop your false specs., shave
the moustache, dye your hair black
instead of blonde, and you're near
enough.'

Now I knew why Mr J. Bull of
D.H.S.S. had to be earnest, honest,
blonde, moustached and bespectacled. If
I had already met our killer he would not
link me with Corelli.

'The other point,' said Stone, 'is that
Corelli's just completed a long stretch,
not as long as demanded by the
prosecution, but long. His old acquain-
tances may well not recognise him;
probably won't want to.'

'And we'll get round that difficulty
anyway,' said Frimmer. 'Shortly after we
put you into circulation you'll get
yourself involved is some minor offence
and go under cover for a few weeks.
That'll break the chain if anyone
from Corelli's past tries to find you.
You'll resurface in another part of
the country, and your whereabouts

conveyed very discreetly to all on our suspect list. A local editor I know will, in hope of a scoop later, prepare me six copies of his rag with a special front page to include your photo. And guess what?'

'Corelli's got no family?' suggested Douglas.

'Right,' said Frimmer, grinning. 'So while we hold him in a safe house Bull can replace him. Also, Bull can listen to some tapes we'll be making so he can practise the accent. Put your skill as mimic to proper use, my lad. Yes, I know about that, been told you do a very scurrilous version of me.'

'You do *accept* the value of bait?' said Stone.

'Of course I do, sir. Just that I expected to be holding the *other* end of the rope.'

'More exciting this way,' said Frimmer, maliciously. 'And it'll help with the A.C. and his budgets.'

'You mean I'll earn my higher salary as a Detective Sergeant?'

'Better than that, Bull. With someone as good as you in the hot seat I don't need to arrange a lot of back-up. You can think of it as holding both ends of the same rope.'

Inevitably, Frimmer had his own appropriate phrase. 'Sacrificial Bull.'

Part Two

Closing In

7

Harry Donaldson is a fair man. Ask him. As he tells you his bushy aircrew moustache banks gently port to starboard. But something about him convinces that flying experience is limited: a package tour to Majorca and he was airsick both ways. Moustache almost hides curled lip as he stares down at the short swarthy man facing him.

'Pity your hair's not grown a bit more, Corelli.' Corelli nods, stifles a sigh. 'I mean — ' says Donaldson, china-blue eyes narrowing — 'I mean, if I give you a job on one of my forecourts my customers'll know you're an ex-con.'

For the first time Corelli looks directly at him, smiles gently into his fat face. 'Sorry, Mr Donaldson.' Both know his hair will soon grow. That smile discomforts Donaldson.

'Well — look here. I mean. Got the business to think of.' And indeed he has: a chain of garages; an empire built on crooks and crookedness. Corelli has come to the right place. 'Well, seeing as I've had a letter from Rehab., and that new probation officer looked in to mention you, it seems you're worth a chance. Being Whitsun, business is picking up. So I'll tell you what. Give you a week's trial here in this garage where I can keep an eye on you.' He strokes his moustache. It banks to port. 'Go out and find Ted Rodgers my manager here. He'll get you set up with a white coat.'

'Thank you, Mr Donaldson.'

'Er — you got somewhere to live?'

'Yes, Mr Donaldson. The welfare got me a room.'

'All right for you,' says Donaldson, sourly. 'You lot can get rooms any time. Decent people go on waiting-lists. Get out before I change my mind!'

Corelli slips out of the office. Little rat, thinks Donaldson. Still, does no harm being known as a fair bloke with the ex-cons. Might lead to business later. Never know who Corelli was working for before going inside. Donaldson smiles.

Ted Rodgers'll bleed the poor wop dry.

Corelli is a hard worker. Rodgers is surprised he is so fit after serving a stretch. Not that fitness counts; what matters is getting him working at the pumps. That is where Rodgers expects to make money out of him.

The other staff accept Corelli good-naturedly enough. They pull his leg over his refusal to take the extra five minutes over a cuppa or a wad. But the leg-pulling is guarded. The haircut, the suggestion of wiriness under the dirty white coat, keep them and their curiosity in check. And they can afford to wait, to see how Rodgers makes Corelli jump. No one is sufficiently interested in Corelli himself to notice that whatever job he happens to be doing at the time he always drifts onto the forecourt at exactly 2 p.m. every day.

Pay day at this garage is Thursday. Donaldson, who enjoys reminding employees he is proprietor, supervises payment in the manager's office. Rodgers handles the pay-packets and the men are called in one at a time.

'Corelli's next,' says Rodgers.

'Right,' says Donaldson. 'Let's see how it goes.'

'Corelli!' bawls Rodgers.

The man appears, stands hesitant in the doorway. He knows trouble.

'Well, come in then,' says Donaldson, moustache straight and level, blue eyes shining. 'Enjoyed your first three days? Good. Sign for your money. Bet you need it!'

Corelli bends over the desk, pen in hand. Rodgers pushes the pay packet across the desk and under the man's nose. Corelli straightens, looks at Donaldson, then Rodgers.

'Bloody sign then,' says Donaldson, grinning.

'What's the matter, wop?' says Rodgers, harshly, his scowl dragging his widow's peak almost to the bridge of his nose.

'This is for sixteen pounds, thirty pence, Mr Donaldson.'

'He can read, Mr Donaldson,' says Rodgers.

'What about it?' asks Donaldson, still grinning.

'That's nearly fourteen pounds short of

what Mr Rodgers agreed with me.' Corelli speaks in a neutral tone. Even on half-pay he needs the job.

'Ah, that's to cover losses at the pumps. Accounts make up the wages, but Mr Rodgers has to deduct what's lost.' Corelli makes no reply but looks steadily at Donaldson. 'You're not suggesting a fiddle, are you?' Donaldson looks sideways at Rodgers. 'You reckon he's suggesting a fiddle, Ted?'

'What him, an ex-con? Nar, Mr Donaldson. He ain't suggestin' no such thing.'

'You stopped Joe a quid,' says Corelli, quietly. 'And that was out of a full week.'

'But he didn't complain,' says Donaldson.

'No, Mr Donaldson. I'm just asking why I'm docked so much more. And I've only worked the three days since Monday.'

'Well, Ted,' says Donaldson, 'explain to the man.'

'Like this, wop,' says Rodgers, folding his arms across his paunch. 'You're the new boy. That means you make more mistakes. You pay more of the loss. On the other hand, you might get extra next week if I think the petrol take's too big.' Rodgers and Donaldson both laugh.

'You mean if I overcharge motorists a total of fourteen pounds next week I can have my right money?'

Rodgers jumps up, steps round the desk, grabs Corelli by the right shoulder. 'Watcher mean, right money? This is *your* right money. And you've picked up a few tips. What's an ex-con like you gotta grouse about?'

'Even in the prisons no one laid hands on me,' says Corelli, softly, looking into Rodgers' face. Slowly, Rodgers lifts his hand off Corelli's shoulder. Unfortunately, Donaldson laughs.

'You've been told, Ted. Told by a little wop!' He has no idea how much trouble will come from this stupid remark.

Corelli sighs. He takes up the pen again, signs his name, pockets the money. As he walks from the office he knows with what expression Rodgers is looking at his back.

On the forecourt all is disappointment.

No explosion has occurred. But, for the moment, Corelli is still impressive enough for others to leave alone. Meanwhile, his colleagues wait for a lead from the manager. Corelli has Friday off, Rodgers has Saturday. On Sunday Rodgers tightens the screws.

He orders Corelli to clean his new Jaguar for him, then complains loudly about the result. Corelli looks at him across the glittering bonnet, but says nothing. This infuriates the manager even more and he orders Corelli to do it again. Corelli knows there is no tip for this job and that he is being kept away from the free-spending Sunday trippers driving onto the forecourt.

Monday is worse. Every job he is set to do he does well, but each time Rodgers criticises the results, refers to 'that convict wop'. By mid-afternoon the atmosphere has become so poisonous that one of the older staff protests to Rodgers. The manager replies offensively, but for the rest of the day contents himself with scowling at Corelli every time he sees him.

As the week progresses Rodgers continues to pick on Corelli. Some of the younger staff, made bold by Corelli's passivity, begin to join in. Returned from lunch, Corelli finds his white coat soaked in petrol. His mug of tea has lavatory paper in it. The wash leather he uses has engine oil spilt on it when his back is turned. But no one touches him — yet.

Wednesday afternoon, 2 p.m., Corelli drifts onto the forecourt although he is supposed to be polishing cars in the showroom. He arrives at the pumps as a black Mercedes draws up. Another attendant serves petrol. Corelli wipes the windscreen. The driver gets out to stretch his legs, removes the driving-glove from his left hand but not the one on his right. He pays the petrol attendant, thanks Corelli, but gives no tip.

'Hard luck, wop,' says the other attendant as the Mercedes rolls forward. Corelli does not appear to hear him. He is staring after the car.

Thursday. Pay day, 11 a.m. Rodgers enjoys playing out the same scene with Corelli as last week. There are only minor changes in the dialogue. Donaldson is not so amused. He half-comprehends that Corelli does not care if the scene replicates what happened last Thursday.

On the forecourt and in the workshop there is bitter disappointment, even disgust. Mutterings about 'lily-livered wops' soon change to plans for 'a bit of horseplay'. Corelli is to be taught a lesson. After lunch is thought to be a good time. Hostility apparently makes no impression on Corelli. The staff on early lunch drift away. Donaldson and Rodgers are already in the local pub. The workshop is empty. Corelli and two other attendants man the forecourt, deal with telephone messages. His colleagues ignore Corelli, do not notice when he leaves the forecourt.

Corelli stands in the centre of the workshop, hands on hips, enjoying his luck. Behind him the great sliding doors of the workshop have been closed up for the lunch-break. He has the place to himself. Parked in the greasing bay, its magnificent radiator facing him, is Donaldson's vintage Bentley. The car *is*

Donaldson: his respectability, success, money, somehow even his women. On the left of the bay is an iron staircase leading to a first floor gallery and offices. To the right of the bay is a large inspection pit.

Corelli walks into the greasing bay, runs a hand over the glistening bonnet of the Bentley. He releases the handbrake. He walks to the back of the bay, presses the operating button. As the hydraulic lift begins to raise the car Corelli leans against one of the tracks. Smoothly, silently, the rising lift swings through ninety degrees until the Bentley faces toward the inspection pit. Corelli walks back to the control panel. As the lift reaches the same height as the first floor gallery he punches the stop button. Donaldson's car is held aloft, front end overhanging the inspection pit, boot backing onto the gallery. A madman entering the workshop might think Corelli is hoping the Bentley will roll off the lift and fall into the pit. But no one enters the workshop. The quiet hum of the hydraulic lift has not been heard on the forecourt where main road traffic roar numbs the senses.

Silent as a cat, Corelli walks under the lift and across the workshop. Parked on the far side is a line of cars including Rodgers' new automatic Jaguar; the car Corelli has cleaned more than once. The keys are in the ignition. He starts the engine, drives the car slowly across the workshop, parks it with nearside wheels lined up on the centre of the inspection pit. He climbs out then leans through the open door, engages drive and pushes with his full strength against the door pillar.

The car lurches forward below the Bentley, dives down and sideways into the concrete pit. All the lamps and windows on the nearside are shattered as the car slumps into the pit. Screeching of buckled and torn metal fills the workshop.

The car's agony is still echoing as Corelli races to the ladder, climbs to the gallery. He jumps onto the lift, wedges himself between the gallery handrail and the back of the Bentley. His shoulders and arms are on the handrail, feet on the car boot. He begins to rock backward and forward. Down on the workshop floor the two pump attendants stand gaping. One shouts instructions to 'Get Rodgers'. They both run out. Corelli is oblivious to them. He is transformed into a coiled spring. As he rocks, his eyes glaze. When the final explosive thrust of his legs occurs he is pushing away more than the frustrations of this place, this time.

The Bentley lurches forward. As the front wheels run off the lift the underside of the car begins to foul the platform. But Corelli has been strong enough. The car keeps moving, sparks showering off its belly. The nose drops as the weight of the engine drags the car down. The bonnet crunches into and through the roof of the car lying in the pit. For an instant the Bentley is poised vertically in the air, nose grinding through the Jaguar. As the Jaguar collapses completely, the Bentley lurches down and slowly, almost majestically, pitches over onto its roof, smashing upside down into the concrete floor.

Corelli listens to the building pulsating with the re-echoing roar of smashing cars. He is lying on the gallery trying to regain breath and strength after that enormous push. By the time he is able to stand the last shards of glass have come to rest, the last groaning metal panels have ceased to writhe. He staggers down the stairs, leans against the wall. Outside, the hum of traffic; inside, the dripping of liquids within the wrecks. There is not long to wait.

Despite his bulk, it is Rodgers who arrives first, running into the workshop, stopping, staring, unbelieving. Corelli smiles at him. Stuttering, Rodgers lurches forward, raises both arms, clenches fists. Corelli moves in low, chops Rodgers across the throat with the edge of a hand that is like a steel bar, smashes the other hand, palm flat, against Rodgers' chest over the heart.

From the ground, Rodgers looks up at him, not really seeing. He prefers to stay down but is spurred on by running footfalls of his staff, of Donaldson his boss. Not knowing how, Rodgers stands, totters. Corelli, still smiling, clenches his fists together somewhere near his right kidney and brings his locked arms scything forward. The tremendous blow

cuts into Rodgers' paunch, continues
— or so it seems to Rodgers — through
his gut and shatters his spine. Rodgers is
hurled across the workshop by the force
of the blow, slumps unconscious at
Donaldson's feet.

Donaldson does not waste a glance on
him. His eyes are riveted on devastation.
The symbol of his life is a buckled maze
of metals and tubing and dripping
liquids: his body and its blood. Eventually, his eyes find Corelli, see the real
man.

'No,' cries Donaldson, appealingly as
Corelli walks toward him.

'O.K. You watch!' says Corelli. Donaldson nods feebly, gestures at his staff to
keep away; keeps his arms outstretched,
crucified. Corelli bends over Rodgers,
rips the wallet from his jacket. 'I take the
fourteen pounds kept from last week and
the fourteen from this. No more.
Understand?' Donaldson nods again.
Contemptuously, Corelli tosses the wallet
onto the greasy floor, pockets his money.
'I go,' he says.

Donaldson, standing with six other

men, can only nod yet again. They step aside for Corelli. He stares at each of them in turn, his would-be teachers, speaks to Donaldson for the last time.

'You give the police a good description of me, won't you?'

Dumbly, Donaldson nods agreement, then, panic-stricken, shakes his head violently. Neither movement dislodges the two enormous tears seeping down into that luxuriant moustache.

Rodgers, sighing like a baby in sleep, begins to vomit over Donaldson's feet.

Corelli smiles, walks out.

8

The Larches, Belmont Avenue, Browcaister, boasts no such tree but offers a prim tidiness that appeals to Corelli. Rest is to be a major occupation, and he rests best with everything in its place. He is admitted by Mrs Gridley. She is not easily impressed by paying guests, but there is something about this new one that discounts his shabby exterior. Maybe it is the splendid travelling-trunk that arrived yesterday. She tells of the trunk as he follows her upstairs. He is interested to see it for the first time. He knows more about her house than he does the trunk. Green leather, brass-bound, brass-locked and offensively new, it lies at the foot of the bed. He is more surprised by the room, knowing it to be square in plan, not expecting half a pyramid. The room crouches in the eaves at the corner of the house. The two outer walls are only five feet high before the sloping ceilings take over. To reach the sink in the corner even Corelli must crouch. The tall window let into the eaves provides relief; or it will do once he can take down the heavy net curtains. Mrs Gridley leaves him to unpack his trunk.

He takes the new key from his pocket, unlocks the trunk: complete new wardrobe. A few items have been worked on to age them a little. Everything fits. Something suggests a woman's choice; he knows which woman. The clothes he is wearing can all be thrown away. He is still unpacking when Mrs Gridley calls up the stairs. Wearing a new suit he prepares to join his new landlady for morning coffee.

Outside on the landing all is as expected. Unencumbered by landlady or suitcase he can look more closely. A genteel and spacious house, new pin clean. Cheap pictures on the walls, and somewhere downstairs will be a flight of plaster ducks. He steadies himself against the banister. This respectable, prim, belaced house is to be a killing ground?

Mrs Gridley presides in her private sitting-room. The ducks fly diagonally down toward her fluorescent-lit cocktail cabinet. In this room the net curtaining is so heavy the electric light is always needed. My den, she says to anyone who queries. Now is a special occasion: welcoming a new guest.

The adverse effect of his foreign name has been offset by the magnificence of the trunk and by the references thoughtfully included with his original letter. However, further reassurances are welcome.

'Jake is not Italian,' agrees Corelli. 'My father was half English. He died years ago. I was brought up as Italian. I also explain,' says Corelli, 'although I am here to start a new job in Browcaister I will not be taking the job full time for a few days. My hours will be irregular.'

'I will, of course, *give* you a *front-door* key as well as your room key,' says Mrs Gridley. 'But I do like to *lock* the front door at night by eleven-thirty. One of the things my *late* husband insisted on.' She waves an arm toward ranks of photographs half-hidden in the gloom.

Corelli can just make out the features of a small defeated man crushed by his wife's love of emphasis. Corelli realises he is in a shrine, hastily explains that by irregular hours he is thinking of the day not the evening.

Archly, Mrs Gridley leans forward. 'You mean you may be *with* me during the *day*?'

Corelli agrees, explains his intention to practise English lessons in his room. He sits well back in his chair. She is a buxom, carefully preserved but also highly seasoned woman of about sixty. He remembers an old saw about letting your armpits be charmpits.

'You are not *required* to be at your new place of employment?' She senses drama.

'Not for all of every day. That could be difficult for the man I am replacing.'

'Oh, I see. Has he been given *notice*?' asks Mrs Gridley.

'Er — no. He's been promoted — like me.'

'Very nice,' she says, comforted and disappointed. 'You have a family to bring up here, later?'

'No. I'm a bachelor.'

'Ah.' She is even more comforted and

less disappointed. 'You may well find a bride here in Browcaister, Mr Corelli. Perhaps you prefer the *mature* type of woman.'

'Indeed I do!' His vehemence and his smile make her all of a quiver and ups-a-daisy, as she later tells her friend Audrey, next door.

'My *late* husband,' she says, with excessive emphasis, 'left me nicely settled, as you see. But one gets *lonely* at times, doesn't one?'

'Yes,' says Corelli, sipping the excellent coffee.

'I hope you like your room,' she says.

'I do, thank you.'

'Mr Anderson left rather suddenly. A nice man. Been with me two years. I wouldn't normally advertise in a newspaper but he gave me so little notice there was not time to rely on *personal* contacts, you see.'

'I understand,' says Corelli, soothingly.

'Yes. Well, now to *business*, Mr Corelli. Thank you for the cheque with your letter. Unexpected but *helpful*. That will certainly cover a month — as I said in my reply. Now, meals are breakfast and dinner. No midday except Sunday when I do a *nice* salad. Breakfast seven-thirty to eight-thirty, dinner is seven *prompt*. No food or drink *in* your room. You will change your bed linen on Tuesdays, putting your bottom sheet and one pillow case in the linen-bag which I leave on the *landing* Tuesday morning. You are free to make your own arrangements about personal laundry but I *recommend* the same company. I always *insist* that — '

As her voice ploughs through the dusty arable of her trade Corelli floats his mind away. Whatever her petty regulations life here will be a kind of heaven after the squalid existence of the last few weeks. The remarkable change in his fortunes will be enjoyed to the full despite Mrs Gridley. Nor will she inhibit — but what she will not inhibit must wait. That clanging voice has switched to a questioning tone.

'Thank you, Mrs Gridley. No, I don't think there is a question. Now I go out.'

Someone following Corelli would have been puzzled by his behaviour. But no one follows. Corelli walks briskly to the library without having to ask for directions. He applies for a reader's ticket, chooses books. After this purposeful activity he behaves like a clockwork toy in need of rewinding; stuttering through the town, not window shopping but corner stopping. At each corner in the town centre he waits, sometimes to stand and stare, sometimes to lean against a wall and riffle through the pages of a library book. Either Corelli likes standing in the sun or he wants to be seen.

At lunch-time he has a whisky and a sandwich in the King's Head. Then his behaviour changes. He visits the two largest stores, seems more interested in the people than in the goods. He soon identifies the store detectives. They are as conspicuous as Mrs Gridley's formation of diving ducks — and as lively. Corelli returns to the first store he visited. This detective is a little keener, a little more awake than his fellow along the street. Corelli watches him pounce on a tired, middle-aged housewife who has forgotten to pay for her chicken, while two teenage girls walk past and out of the store wearing brand new stolen topcoats.

Corelli walks back to The Larches. Mrs Gridley is at afternoon bingo. He unlocks his own door, throws his jacket on the bed, then silently and systematically enters and searches every other room in the house. The other guests' locked doors all yield to Corelli's keys. He returns to his own room, leaves the door open because of the heat that has built up under the sloping, cramping roof, lies on the bed.

He is sleeping when Mrs Gridley returns. For a moment she stands in the doorway looking down on him. Then she goes to her own room, cheerful despite losses in the bingo hall. Corelli wrinkles his nose, groans softly. *That* complication would be unbearable.

9

'I'll introduce you,' says Mrs Gridley, walking ahead of Corelli into the dining-room.

'Good evening, everyone,' she says. 'I am *pleased* to introduce our new resident, Mr Corelli. Miss Sykes — Mr Corelli. Mr Corelli — Miss Sykes.' He receives a shy almost furtive glance. 'Mr Hammond — Mr Corelli.' A podgy not very steady hand is thrust at him and he is welcomed as 'old boy'. 'Mr Robinson — Mr Corelli.' No words, only the thin limp hand tentatively offered. Corelli sits at the window-table while his fellow-guests shuffle their feet. He suspects introductions have delayed the meal.

There is tomato soup, lamb chop with new potatoes and cabbage, apple pie and custard, coffee. The food is well cooked, served hot, but there is no choice, not even with or without custard. Eating, Corelli surveys the other residents, each sitting at their own table. They are the stuff of boarding-house life.

Miss Sykes — Evelyn — is fortyish in years and hip and bust. (Sexy underwear in her right-hand top drawer, but her wardrobe hangs drab with grey and beige.) She dresses to conceal. Moon-face, slightly puckered over her book. An impression she is never far from tears. Probably known to colleagues at the library as 'poor Evelyn'. Few friends. (There are few letters in her drawer and they are mostly from hurt, bewildered, lonely mummy.) Now, Evelyn lives in the world of romantic novels. (Her cupboard is jammed with such books unofficially borrowed from her work.) Life was not always so. Her share of ordinary human passions may have been banal but the bitterness is sharp enough. (In her small, hollow-rattling jewel box — an engage-ment ring.) She is not turning the pages of her book. She is reconstructing her life to accommodate this Mr Corelli. A new face is a threat until it can be made to resemble other more familiar faces. But the bland, unsalted porridge of her existence cannot easily absorb this stranger: foreign and gypsy-like. She frowns. Gypsy is a category outside her experience and therefore unacceptable. Mr Corelli will remain merely a name until something in his behaviour is recognised. She will be a useless witness.

Albert Hammond is a fifty year old overweight dinosaur fighting for survival. (Under his bed are bathroom scales set to show him half a stone lighter than he is.) He has emerged from swamps where education was cissy, wife-beating was masculine, and widely scattered bastards were signs of virility. The harsh light of today blinds him: rebellious women, contemptuous children, unsympathetic lawyers. (A drawer full of solicitors' letters.) Earning to pay court orders has emasculated him. The sloping forehead and bald dome overlay a mind hopelessly bemused by the battle to exist in this new era. Much of his bemusement has to do with the veins broken in his nose, the unsteadiness of his stubby fingers. (In a bottom drawer the empty bottles lie waiting their turn to be smuggled away.)

And he has lost the salesman's consolation of believing his own sales talk; he is a hewer of wood in a plastic age. Albert Hammond sags.

Frederick Robinson is a highly qualified engineer. (A folder in his top drawer is crisp with degrees and certificates.) His life, sixty aching years, is a wail of undeserved misfortune. Ignoring career prospects he had stayed in the same job while nursing his widowed, bullying mother. After her death it was discovered debts exceeded assets. (He also has a collection of solicitors' letters.) Frederick had moved to a bed-sitter, saved hard, paid off the debts. Then he had become ill and lost his job. The pattern formed, locked round him: new job, victim of the cruelty of last in first out, ill-health, the fight back to another job, then a new redundancy. And there was always a reason why redundancy payment could be cut or withheld. (Carbon copies of all his querulous letters somehow less healthy than Albert's soft porn. magazines.)

Now, reduced to a packer but having worked steadily for twenty months, he has discovered an eczema growing on his hands. (His toilet-bag is full of proprietary treatments.) Because he works in a food factory he dare not go to a doctor. This latest threat and his history of decline, if not already known to Corelli, might be suspected from Frederick's appearance. He is tall, gangling, concave-chested, thin-limbed; a breathing impediment causes his mouth to droop open; rheumy eyes suggest threat of tears; the firm line of the hooked nose is somehow dissipated by the jungly tufts in each nostril; the hairs, like all his hair, white for thirty years. And with the fingers of one hand he picks at the flakes of skin between the fingers of the other. Frederick Robinson: victim.

So be it, thinks Corelli. A victim may be a victim.

Corelli becomes a genial, friendly fellow-guest; stalking like a smiling tiger. Mrs Gridley has a previous engagement, Miss Sykes and Mr Robinson decline for unspecified reasons, but Mr Hammond is delighted to be invited out for a drink. What else is there to do when too tired to get excited by photographs of pubic hair? By 10.30 Albert and Jake are chums. Corelli decides he likes Albert, is glad Frederick Robinson is the target.

Next evening, Corelli continues to charm. He asks how their day went, leads them into individual private exchanges. Miss Sykes, without understanding why, explains she is not to be found in the town centre library when Corelli visits because she works in a small branch out in the country. Mr Robinson suddenly discovers he has admitted to Wednesday afternoons off and stated his preference for Frederick rather than Fred. Albert Hammond can foresee more jolly evenings ahead, as can Mrs Gridley who discovers roses from her new guest placed on a table in her den. She decides she has once again *selected* an excellent *man* to live *with* her. She is charmed by the man and the 'with'.

None of them learn anything of Corelli's first day in Browcaister. He has spent several hours writing in the library. He has taken a late lunch in the Red Lion and met Una, a ravaged blonde. He has gone with her to a flat and discovered her friend, Kathy, in bed. He has had an intimate triangular afternoon.

At The Larches, Corelli is accepted into the little community. As if he had *always* been here, says Mrs Gridley to her friend Audrey. (Behind the lie is concealed a quickening turmoil in the lady's breast.) Audrey is wise enough not to comment, but silently registers the sentimental expression on her neighbour's face. Things are certainly not as they were. An outward sign of inner disturbance is that Mrs Gridley is bathing more often. This brings some relief to all her residents, but they are only half-aware of it. Corelli is also disturbing them. Evelyn Sykes is wearing the lightest of her three grey dresses, attributing this step to the swelling of summer. Albert Hammond sags a little less, is swept up by a new wave of optimism. He and Corelli now go out for drinks most evenings. Companionship leads Albert Hammond into a blurred cheerfulness rather than drunkenness. Frederick Robinson has found in Corelli a sympathetic, unjudging listener;

has even been able to confess to eczema. And there is talk of Corelli finding him a better post in Corelli's new company.

And Corelli? He lies on his bed, face disfigured by a silent scream. No respite from waiting to die. Few outlets for the mind and only that one for the body. Una and Kathy have confessed their fear to each other. It is not the strange pattern of scars on his body that frightens, in fact that adds a frisson to touching and being touched. Their fear is rooted in sensing a far greater, more destructive power lying beneath the strength he expends on them in the great bed. They will only offer themselves as a pair. Alone could be annihilation.

A quiet week-end carries Corelli into a new week that offers actions very different from the skills of Una and Kathy. Monday morning, in the street, he is delighted by someone else's misfortune. A tall, burly man who looks like a policeman is struggling to change a wheel on his car. Corelli approaches, whistling.

'Good morning,' says Corelli. 'Looks like you might need some help.'

'Sod off!' says the big man, grinning.

'Certainly,' says Corelli. 'When?'

'This week. Bugger!' The expletive is directed at the collapsed jack rather than Corelli.

'Wednesday,' says Corelli, and walks away happy to wait for Wednesday.

Frederick Robinson also awaits Wednesday, his halfday. When it comes he is surprised and pleased that his new fellow-guest has the afternoon off as well. Corelli suggests they meet after lunch for a shared shopping expedition. What he is about to do is sufficiently repugnant for him not to want to eat with the victim.

When they meet Corelli manœuvres them into the store with the keenest detective. He suggests they shop separately to avoid waiting too long for each other to complete their different purchases. Robinson has no objection to this arrangement, enjoys the companionship implicit in the way he and Corelli keep meeting as they cross each other's tracks from department to department. He is unaware of the other meeting: Corelli and the store detective, the sly accusation, the pointing finger. When his shopping is completed he sees Corelli near the shop doorway. Apparently, Corelli does not see him but walks out into the street. Robinson hurries after him. As the doors close behind him a stranger, face distorted by excitement, steps up to him.

Corelli enjoys his evening meal, expresses regret to Mrs Gridley that Robinson is not well enough to come down. After dinner Corelli goes upstairs, knocks on the door labelled F.R. No reply. Alarmed, Corelli knocks again. To his relief Robinson opens the door. He is ashen, confused, wishes to be left alone. Corelli ignores the signals, pushes into the room, asks where Robinson got to during the afternoon; explains he lost sight of him in the store and decided to come home.

Slumped on the bed, struggling for breath between tears, Robinson tells his shameful story. Incomprehensible. A pair of socks in his pocket and he had never seen them before. How could this be so? And the store detective had also checked his bag: three items had not been registered on the till receipt. Two of them were small tins of fruit.

'What would I want with those when I have evening meals with Mrs Gridley?' The heart-rending cry brings from Corelli a sharp response.

'Not any more you don't, Frederick!'

'What?'

'The best thing you can do is move out now. Avoid a scandal, avoid this getting back to your place of work. Let the police have your new address so they don't call here or at work.'

'But where — '

Amazingly, Corelli knows where, can arrange in the morning. He produces a 'sleeping pill' to help through the night. The pill completes the collapse. By the time the effects have worn off Robinson has slept, has had breakfast, surrendered his wallet to Corelli to pay off Mrs Gridley, has had his bags packed by Corelli, been taken in a taxi by Corelli to the far side of town, to digs run by a muscular young woman who seems to regard Corelli as God. This opinion Robinson is inclined to share. Such positive concern, such caring from another person is a new experience in his non-experienced life. Even the final brutality is acceptable, explicable.

'I think I must withdraw my offer to find you a new job,' says Corelli. 'It's hardly possible for me to introduce a shop-lifter into my new firm.'

Tears streaming, Robinson agrees. He also understands why he will not meet Corelli again. Somehow the rejections are justified because they come from a man so caring. And as a last favour Corelli will telephone Robinson's place of work and explain he is unwell today. As Robinson burrows his face into the pillow, pulls the sheet over his head, he releases his fingerhold on belief in his own innocence. In Corelli's compassion he sees confirmation of guilt. Some kind of mental blackout must have possessed him while shopping, perhaps something to do with anxieties about the eczema and losing the job. And he did have those items in his possession. But now, thanks to Corelli, he does not have to face the reproachful eyes of Evelyn Sykes and Mrs Gridley when the police call. And he might even keep his job.

Corelli's compassion for his fellow-man apparently travels with him back to The Larches where he pacifies Mrs Gridley, insists on handling the advert for the empty room. Mrs Gridley is content. Her Mr Corelli seems to know what he is about.

Lying on his bed Corelli does know what he is about. He is securing his emotions, battening down against a roaring sea of self-disgust. Eventually, he will be able to use necessity as justification, but until that becomes possible for him he is in danger of being swamped by his own feelings. The sloping roof crouching over his bed resonates with a kind of rage.

10

Days passing like grief bring yet another Monday. Walking to the library, Corelli, beginning to feel a familiar body language, knows he is being followed. He stops and stares into a shop window, sees his face suffused with a mixture of excitement and relief. This will not do. He slows his breathing, waits for the blood to check its flood. Behind him the cardboard figures of townsfolk hurry to work or morning shopping. None is projected three-dimensionally. Enduring ignorance, he completes his journey to the library and barricades himself behind books in the reference room. He is in a dilemma. He wants to know which fish he has caught, but attempts to find out might frighten off the catch. He must continue to play the line; a dangerous game when each believes the other is the prey. How dangerous that game is Corelli will soon discover.

Lunchtime he is not followed. Perhaps his tail has only to locate him in the morning. So what else happens in the morning? Has someone called at The Larches, left a package, searched his room? 'The Gas Man Cometh,' mutters Corelli, almost jovial with expectations of action. He moves on to an afternoon with Una and Kathy. They find him unusually light-hearted; a mood contradicting the brooding sense of threat that has troubled them before. Wise in their trade they say nothing, but their bodies move easily today. He is doubly upset that this is the one day he must leave them earlier than usual.

Back at The Larches he shares the cool hall with Mrs Gridley's hall furniture. Meanwhile, in some other larger broiling hall, Mrs Gridley places her counters, hopes for a win. Wishing her well, Corelli searches every room on the ground floor. In the dining-room laid tables wait. In the den the petrified ducks cling to the wall. Only in the kitchen is there life. On a sunlit plate groaning meat stealthily thaws for dinner.

Avoiding the squeaky third and fifth steps, Corelli arrives on the landing. If someone is waiting for him up here they will expect him to go first to his own room or the lavatory. Silently, he lets himself into Mrs Gridley's room. No disarray. He listens at the wall between her room and his. He waits, shirt sticking in his armpits. Nothing. Then he searches every other room, his own last of all. And still nothing. He hurls his damp clothes onto his bed, then runs yet another bath Mrs Gridley won't know about.

That evening, after dinner, Corelli makes his excuses to disppointed Albert and sets out for the pub by himself. The tail is there again.

Nursing his drink in the saloon bar of The Goat Corelli unpacks his recollections of the day. He suspects his own scheming is an insignificant strand in the larger web others are weaving round him. He feels stifled, his breathing restricted by something more oppressive than the heat of the night. He leaves the bar and stands in the street sweating. A tracery of distant thunder is appropriate. He moves on to

The Vine, beginning the slow pub crawl that drags his follower across most of Browcaister. A part of Corelli enjoys the thought of someone tired and thirsty being unable to follow him into any of the bars. He decides to follow an indirect route back to Mrs Gridley's if only to keep his tail in suspense. Corelli makes this mistake not because he is drunk, which he is not, but because another part of him is disoriented by stress: stress that has been accumulating in him over the weeks like a powerful electrical charge.

In a maze of little back streets Corelli pauses and listens. Somewhere beyond the dying traffic noise someone else may be standing and listening. Corelli crushes the desire to turn back and rush yelling into the darkness. The last thing he wants is to flush out his tail; he needs that companionship more than he needs to satisfy his intense curiosity. Corelli walks on. Hearing no footsteps behind him he wonders if his tail has slipped ahead along some parallel street. Maybe there is more than one tail and he is sandwiched between them. Suddenly, his defenceless-ness hurts like a body pain. What if he has misread the intentions of all these other people? Is it possible he is required to die tonight?

Beneath a flickering ochre street lamp he crouches, tightens a shoelace. Running may be his only defence. A car rolls slowly past, radio music drifts out onto the pavement. Corelli starts walking again under the red-black sky. He feels cold. Twenty yards ahead a quiet crossroads is waiting. Aware of high hedge corners he sets out to cross the junction diagonally. Obsessed with detecting footsteps perhaps he misses other sounds.

He is a third of the way across the road and the unlit car is upon him. He dives, rolls, somehow scrapes his way over the crown of the road and down into the far gutter. The car skids past his flailing legs and swings away up the next side street. Lying in the gutter, listening to the engine roaring across the night, he hears another sound. Somewhere someone is running — and running away.

Corelli drags himself onto the pavement, sits with his back against a garden wall. In several houses curtains are pulled aside at lighted windows, front doors bang. Corelli sits perfectly still in the darkness. He wants no assistance, no inquiries. Doorstep conversations die. Reluctantly, curtains swing back, night-bolts slide. Real life has not lived up to T.V. Slowly, Corelli checks his limbs, his back, his neck. Nothing broken but plenty of cuts and bruises. Shock expresses itself initially in sorrowing over the trousers he will never be able to wear again. Warm blood begins tackily to hold the ripped cloth against his knee. He will have to move soon or face the painful task of unsticking the wound. He manages to stand for a moment, then sits back on top of the low wall. As his mind regains control he recognises the full significance of what has happened. Someone wants him dead — but it is not his tail.

Corelli tries to rerun the incident in his mind, is ashamed so little can be recalled. The car must have been rolling fast with the clutch in. Then that tremendous

122

acceleration almost caught him. The car was dark, perhaps black. Something about the driver. That blurred shape glimpsed as he had dived sideways across the road. Yes. The driver was small, not just crouched, but small. And so skilful. Must have tried that trick before, perhaps successfully. And those running footsteps? Heavy, long strides. Almost certainly a man able to move fast.

Corelli stands upright, winces as weight falls on his knee-joints. But he has to move now he knows he is a target. Any car may swerve onto the pavement. Ruefully acknowledging new implications of waiting being over, he limps through the June night keeping close to walls and away from kerbs. When he has to cross a road he does so well away from corners and parked cars. He fears his increased alertness is now offset by the effects of his injuries.

At The Larches he works his way up the side of the drive so he is not silhouetted against the hall light. Key in hand he scurries into the porch, then into the hall and safety. Is it safety? He looks at the board. He is the only one out. Keeping clear of the glass panel in the front door he edges the door-catch into place. Outside Mrs Gridley's den he listens to her harsh voice as she sings over her final gin. He checks every other room in the house, listens to the night sounds of Albert's snores, Evelyn's soft breathing. Their doors are safely locked. By the time Corelli has once again satisfied himself no stranger is in the house, no death-trap set, his cuts have congealed and perspiration dried to a clammy glaze. Defying a brand new notice to the contrary, he runs yet another hot bath and painfully submerges himself in it. He must be in good shape for tomorrow. Whatever Tuesday brings will have something to do with today, and today he nearly died.

11

Tuesday brings a headache, sore shoulder, bruised elbows, pains in cut knees, and the problem of disposing of a torn suit. The day also bring questions from Mrs Gridley about late night baths. Fortunately, Evelyn looks so furtive and Albert so stupid, Corelli is not suspected. But Mrs Gridley has other questions.

'Whose brown paper parcel is that in my *hall*?' she asks, slamming down toast.

'Er — mine, Mrs Gridley,' says Corelli. 'Some old clothes I want to take to the Oxfam shop.'

'Pity, Mr Corelli. If you let me have them I'll find a *good* home for them.'

'Thank you for the offer but I'm taking them into town after breakfast.'

'And what about Mr Robinson's *room*?' Corelli's hand is nearly crushed by the coffee-pot.

'I'm going to the newspaper office this

afternoon to see if we've any replies to the advert.'

'I do hope you know what you're *doing*, Mr Corelli. I can't afford to leave that room empty for weeks and weeks.' Mrs Gridley steams out, still quivering.

'Bad lad,' says Albert, from the other side of the dining room.

'Whaddya mean?' snaps Corelli. His left knee is giving him hell.

'You're not exactly courting the lady, are you?' says Albert, grinning. Evelyn expresses her disgust at this remark by rattling her coffee-cup on the saucer and leaving the room to fetch the morning paper. 'There's another,' says Albert, giggling. 'Dunno how you do it, Jake. Woman like honey bees.' So poetic a vision suggests Albert has already broached a bottle today.

'My charm,' says Corelli, and neatly decapitates his boiled egg, a trick Albert's twitching hands cannot emulate. Evelyn returns with her newspaper, hides behind it.

Limping into town, brown-paper parcel under his arm, briefcase in hand, Corelli feels defenceless. There is no sign of a tail, but perhaps he is being watched from a window or from a parked car. Just before he reaches the town centre he stops at a litter bin and stuffs the parcel into it. Carefully, he crosses the road. The library seems to be a very long way away.

He pushes through the swing doors of the library and enters the lending section. He is a familiar figure now, and the pert brunette, pointy breasts flattened by an armful of books, gives him her best smile. He gravely inclines his head. 'Women like honey bees?' He crosses to the staircase in the far corner of the section and climbs to the reference library on the first floor. In the corner are the two old men who arrive promptly at 9.30 every morning to share the day with each other and with the young beauties in the photographic magazines on the periodical racks. The bearded librarian in attendance stares at the row of pencils blunted for him by the public yesterday. Angrily, he pokes a pencil into the sharpening machine. The room is filled with an irritating grinding noise symbolic of the British at their books.

Corelli limps down the gangway between the desks toward what he now regards as his desk. He stops, stares. On the desk is the brown-paper parcel he had dumped in the litter bin a few minutes ago. The old men mutter over the models. The pencil sharpener grinds on.

Painfully, Corelli lowers himself onto the chair, puts his briefcase on the floor. He inspects the parcel. It is undoubtedly his parcel. The pencil sharpener stops. The bearded youth wipes his glasses with a dirty hand-kerchief. He needs a break from the toughest job in a librarian's day. Very slowly, he walks along the gangway to Corelli.

'You are Mr Corelli, aren't you?'

'That's right.' Corelli smiles.

'Your friend said you were expecting that parcel. I let 'im leave it because he seemed to know you so well. Very good description he gave.'

'I'm sure,' says Corelli, drily. 'And thank you so much for your help.' He knows that rules, real and imaginary, have

128

been broken on his behalf.

Corelli puts the parcel on the floor under the desk, nudges it affectionately with his toes. Somewhere out on the streets somebody is looking after him, somebody with an instantly recognisable sense of humour. A pity he wasn't available last night, thinks Corelli. He is aware that the two old men are staring at him, sucking their teeth disapprovingly. He is humming to himself! He nods at them, rests his head on his arms and falls asleep. Interminable morning and a long, slow lunch bring him to afternoon. The only diversion is replacing his parcel in the same waste bin.

The main business of the afternoon is concerned with Mrs Gridley's new lodger. At the newspaper office Corelli is handed four letters from people wanting Frederick Robinson's room. Sitting on a bench against the wall he studies the envelopes. Inside one of them is a letter from his executioner.

'Are you all right, sir?' The office lad fixes him with glittering eyes. He knows that box numbers can bring a little drama into life. The gentleman does not want to open his letters.

'Yes, thank you,' says Corelli, turning the envelopes. One of them bears no stamp, was delivered by hand. He knows at once it is the letter he has been waiting for. Perversely, he opens the other three first. Three innocent letters: clumsy, anxious to please. He throws them into the waste bin but puts the self-addressed envelopes in his pocket. He will be writing to them telling them they were unlucky.

The fourth letter is correct in style but contains an envelope addressed to a box number. Almost reluctantly he drags his thumb off the bottom of the perfectly typed letter and exposes the signature: Miss Jean Hutchinson.

As one part of his mind grapples with the writer's sex another struggles with the name.

He telephones Mrs Gridley. 'We have a reply,' he says, lying by omission. A time is arranged for the interview. He returns to the bench, scribbles a reply to Miss Hutchinson, puts it in her envelope, hands the letter to the office boy with the money for the phone call.

The boy is delighted that Corelli does not immediately walk out but returns again to the bench. Corelli sits for some time and thinks about box numbers. A stake-out is possible, but for what purpose? If she realises she is being watched everything is lost, and he will be meeting her anyway. Meeting her? Did they almost meet last night? The sense of being stifled that was with him then suddenly returns and intensifies. It is as if someone immensely strong is slowly, almost casually crushing him to death.

For the first time he doubts his ability to continue alone. He is grateful that the joke with the parcel was played this morning. Stiffly, he stands up, walks out into summer sunshine.

In the evening Corelli receives further support from a different source. Mrs Gridley hands him a letter as he enters the dining room.

'Came after you left this morning, Mr Corelli. Your *first* since you came here, isn't it?'

'Yes. Er — it's from my mother.'

'With an English stamp?'

'She doesn't live in Italy. She lives in Stoke Newington — in London. I do telephone her every week, you know,' he says, defensively.

Mrs Gridley sweeps out to fetch the soups. Corelli reads his letter.

'Nothing wrong, dear?' asks Mrs Gridley, hopeful as ever, putting his soup in front of him.

'No, nothing's wrong. She's just a bit lonely that's all — being a widow.'

'Oh, I do so *understand* how she feels. I really *do*. I'm sure she'll be glad to see you when you can get away from your new job. But I hope you won't go the day this Miss Hutchinson is coming?'

'No. I'll be here for that. Maybe I go home at the weekend.'

Mrs Gridley bridles somewhat. She would like Jake Corelli to refer to The Larches as home. Never mind, she thinks, boys good to their mothers are usually good to their wives. And that's all you know, thinks Corelli, reading her mind.

'What's this about a Miss Hutchinson?'

gulps Albert, through a filter of soup, as Mrs Gridley closes the dining room door. Evelyn's right hand stops turning the pages of her book.

'She may be the new guest in place of Frederick Robinson. She answered the newspaper advert.'

'Getting another woman in, eh?' says Albert, spraying soup, nodding approvingly. Evelyn wears her usual disgusted expression.

'Not necessarily,' says Corelli, coldly. 'She's only one applicant. There may be others more suitable, including men.' Unaware of what she is doing, Evelyn nods.

Thursday afternoon, three o'clock. Corelli and Mrs Gridley stand side by side in the entrance hall of The Larches.

'Don't know why I'm so nervous this time,' says Mrs Gridley, plaintively.

Corelli loosens the knot of his tie, wishes he looked shabbier. Wearing a grubby shirt is not sufficient evidence of criminality. But it is his face this caller will inspect.

'Take my arm,' says Corelli.

Hesitantly, Mrs Gridley does so, immediately feels worse.

Footsteps on gravel.

'Listen!' She gasps the word. 'Must be her. Give me a minute before you show her into the den.' Patting her hair, Mrs Gridley trots into her room, leaves the door slightly ajar.

Standing alone, Corelli watches the front door. A human outline begins to form and enlarge, become partially defined through the frosted glass. The outline is feminine, as is the gesture of raising the hand to the bell-push. The shriek of the bell shatters the frosted panes and Corelli sees the face of the woman in the porch. But the glass is unchanged. It is his mind's eye that has been cleared by that gesture.

Slowly, Corelli opens the door. He steps aside and she walks in. Her eyes have darkened with the shock of recognition. Immediately above the bridge of her nose a slight frown creases the centre of her forehead. Is she wondering if she knows him in some other sense of knowing? The clamorous jostling of her many feelings is almost audible, yet she and Corelli confront each other like deaf mutes.

Corelli could share some of her feelings. They are those which a policeman has when, having read all the files, he meets his suspect for the first time. Just as a photograph never quite conveys movement so written words never fully portray the living subject. There is always a mismatch between the reality of the person and the words. But a greater mismatch has silenced him. He knows they are not meeting for the first time. She does not.

Part Three

Ordinary Human Passions

Ordinary Human Passions

12

Night rain had pock-marked the open top deck of the car park with puddles not yet evaporated by Monday morning sun. Rain-washed graffiti on the concrete parapets invited me to perform impossible tasks. Some were impossible because I was breathless. The lifts were not working and I had run up the six flights of stairs. Had anyone been following me they must have died somewhere about the fourth floor.

Detective Sergeant Jim Douglas leaned against the parapet on the far side of the deck and looked across central Birmingham.

'Makes the Bomb seem redundant, don't it?' he said, nodding his head at the view as I slumped next to him. A cooling breeze stung my face like aftershave. I took several deep breaths.

' 'One has no great hopes from Birmingham. I always say there is something direful in the sound,' ' I said.

Jim looked at me. He knew it was a quotation but could not place it. He also knew I knew he could not place it and was not going to help him.

'Morning, Jack,' he said.

'Thank you for your letter, Mother.'

'This seemed a good place to meet. We'd know if you were followed — specially as we switched off the lifts.' I was still too breathless to curse him. He nudged me with his shoulder. 'Do I call you Corelli or Bull?'

'Call me what you like. I'm so knackered I'll answer to anything. Strain of all this acting.'

For a moment we listened to my breathing and the melancholy sounds of the city at work.

'Now you know who our killer is do you know who you are?' he said, slowly.

'I look at myself in the hall mirror when I come down to breakfast, and under my breath I say: 'Good morning, Jake Corelli.' That's all it takes.'

'Liar.'

'Yes.' I stared at a giant tombstone

masquerading as a multi-storey office block. 'The other thing is the waiting. But that's nearly over now — one way or the other.'

'Yeah. Perhaps you'll only be Corelli for a few more days. Better make the most of it! Say something in your Italian voice, go on.' He nudged me again.

'Ah, shut up!'

'Sounded just like Detective Sergeant Jack Bull to me,' said Jim. We both thought about Detective Sergeant Jack Bull for a moment. 'Feel a bit more committed now you know who tried to run you down?'

'You bugger,' I said, bitterly. 'It was you following me. And then you bloody ran off.'

'So what? When I saw you rolling in the gutter I knew you'd woken up enough to look after yourself if the driver had a second go.' I glared at him. 'Whaddya expect me to do, come and dust you down? You don't think anyone's going to risk blowing the set-up at this stage, after all our hard work? You knew you were on your own and you're old enough to cross the street by yourself. Probably did you good to get shaken up a bit.' He allowed me a little time to sulk. 'Aw, come on, Jack! Next thing is you'll want her charged with one attempted murder instead of with fourteen successful ones.'

I turned away and watched a battered Ford lurch past us. A dark-haired woman with a face like a wasp was steering with one hand while slapping her child about the head with the other. She was the first driver to park on the top deck. She was going to be even more waspish when she found out about the lifts. We watched her lock the car and then drag the child and her shopping baskets into the exit tower. Jim turned back to me.

'Anyhow, as soon as Frimmer gave the say-so, I *did* tip you off that I was back again. We knew who we were after by that time, so we knew when it was safe to make another contact with you.'

'Oh, I guessed *that* was you as soon as I saw the parcel on the desk. Been waiting for you to surface again ever since I saw you changing the wheel of that car. But I'd no idea you were also my tail.'

'I'm annoyed with myself you ever knew you had one.'

'I score a team point there, do I?'

'Small triumphs for small men I say.' He looked down at me. 'But never mind, Jack, everything's falling into place now, thank God. We all had a nasty moment wondering if she'd get Robinson's old room. Just possible Mrs Gridley might've taken a strong dislike to her and turned her down.'

'Not very likely. She wanted the room rented out again and she believed me when I said there was only one applicant. All I had to do was make the right noises about that applicant: comment on her income rather than her face, on her respectability rather than her legs. Very keen on respectability is my Mrs Gridley, I'm glad to say. She suffers from a sort of respectable lustfulness, restricts her advances to innuendoes I can ignore. If she started being direct and leaping into my bed I think that would be the end of me — in several senses.'

'Can't have that, Jack. You're there to

die for another woman not for your landlady!'

'At least she's more attractive than Mrs Gridley.'

'And a damn'd sight more dangerous.'

'No need to tell me.'

'Miss Grey didn't recognise you?'

'Course she did!'

'What do — '

'As Jake Corelli not as Jack Bull. She was all prepared to recognise me but conditioned to recognise me as Corelli. She just wasn't functioning in a way that allowed any link with that ineffectual Mr Bull of D.H.S.S.'

'You could have problems with other women, Jack. Orders from Frimmer include one saying you're to stop seeing those two tarts.' Jim looked away from me.

Momentarily, I was back in the big bed: Una blonde, older; Kathy brunette, younger. Not just sex, beginning to like, to enjoy them, their tough humour. Three outcasts together?

'I guess you had to report *everything* you found out, Jim. But is Frimmer

144

worried by morals or money?'

'Don't be bloody silly! Of course he's bothered by the amount you're costing us, but he's a damned sight more bothered that your connection with those women might foul up the operation in some way.'

'It's all part of being in rôle as Corelli.'

'Tell Frimmer your own lies, Jack. I'm not.'

'Let's change the subject, Jim. Did all six of our suspects get fake copies of the local paper with my picture in it?'

'They did. In most cases by pretending an incorrect delivery: wrong house number or wrong street. No copies returned to local newsagents. Shows how dishonest our readers are. All right! Don't look so suspicious. We all knew it might be hit and miss. But we didn't have that problem with Madelaine Grey, and if she's got accomplices she would've told 'em where Corelli is.'

'Why don't you have that problem with her?'

Jim looked shifty. I guessed Frimmer had made a change in our plans without bothering to tell me.

'We've put someone in West House and they made sure she saw the paper.'

'That's all I need. Who?'

'Detective Inspector Susan Green.' I stared at him. Somewhere in the city an ambulance cried its way through the streets. 'They've become quite good friends,' said Jim, defensively.

'I bet! And Frimmer's worried my two little tarts might complicate things.' Jim looked down over the parapet. I kept my teeth in the same bone. 'Has old man Johnson rumbled her?'

'No reason to think so.'

'Think so! You hang my life on a 'think so'?'

'Knock it off, Jack! What's all this holier than thou stuff? Just because you've got a thing about Green don't mean to say Frimmer doesn't know what he's doing.'

'Let me tell you — '

'No, Jack. Don't tell me! I'm just the messenger boy. Save it all for Frimmer. And another thing: just remember the point of that job at the garage was to introduce a break in Corelli's life between leaving prison and getting to The Larches. The minor incident you were supposed to cause was merely a stop if our suspect checked back on you via that press photo. Mayhem was *not* required.'

'You think not? Well, call it therapeutic!'

'I think I'm beginning to feel sorry for our murderer.'

'Don't be! That could be my mistake. Meanwhile, I'm only emulating the real Corelli, aren't I? Don't confuse him with me. How is the poor bugger, anyway?'

'Low. He was picked up as soon as he reached the street. We made it look right with uniformed men in a Panda. Started by questioning him about some minor offences left on the books. He's deteriorating fast now. The shock of losing freedom as soon as he thought he'd got it. On top of that he knows he's being held in a safe house and not a prison or remand centre. And there are no other prisoners to associate with. A week ago he made an escape attempt, but now he seems to be a broken man. Just sits quiet in his cell. In the exercise periods he sits out in the yard, won't talk with the guards. The doctor's beginning to make concerned noises about him.'

'And I think *I'm* trapped.'

'There's always someone worse off — '

'Stuff it! O.K., O.K. I'm sorry. Just been having a rough — '

He raised his hand, silenced me. On the deck below us tyres screeched. Someone was driving too fast. Jim stepped away from me, casually undid the button of his jacket, folded his arms so that his right hand vanished inside the coat. I felt the rough edge of the parapet snag my clothing as I turned. Behind us the ground, and Jim's back-up, were six floors down.

The car raced up the ramp, swerved toward us, then swung in a complete circle before roaring out of the exit. The four youths inside were yelling and laughing. One of us sighed.

'Should we tell a policeman?' asked Jim, unfolding his arms, buttoning his jacket.

'Never find one when you want one,' I said, shrilly.

The way Jim had unbuttoned his coat had shaken me almost as much as that hit-and-run attempt. Suddenly, my whining about Frimmer, and his about me, were trivial in relation to our shared objective.

'So what exactly are my instructions?' I asked. 'Miss Madelaine Grey moved in last night.'

13

Summoned by the dinner-gong I came out of my room on Monday evening and found her waiting for me.

'Good evening, Miss Hutchinson,' I said.

'Good evening, Mr Corelli.' She stared at me, then pulled her door shut. She walked past me to the top of the stairs. A fragrant woman dressed entirely in brown. 'Please call me Madelaine.'

'I — er — ' I said. She stopped with the line of her hips tilted away from me, her long right leg poised over the first step down, slim hand on the banister. 'Er — I thought Mrs Gridley said your name was Jean.'

'It is, but I prefer my middle name.' Her face came alive with a smile that might have ravished me when we had first met.

'Oh, yes. I'm Jake.'

As I followed her down the stairs I

could have put out my hand and touched the shining crown of her head or lifted the supple brown hair from her collar. Then, had she stopped, I might have leaned down and kissed the nape of her neck. Within her head sparked the same wonderful chemistry that is every human mind but it had programmed the output of a common criminal. Madelaine! She wanted me to know her real name for the same reason some crooks send anonymous notes to the police, and arsonists watch their own fires.

During dinner I did not speak to my fellow-guests. While Madelaine and Evelyn exchanged small talk, or while they both humoured Albert by laughing politely at his sallies, I scowled at my food and struggled with conflicting feelings. On one hand was relief that our suppositions were now supported by some realities. (Too soon to talk of evidence, but a suspect had stepped into the clearing.) On the other hand was regret. I wanted to lead her back to West House, keep her permanently confined in safe, familiar quietness.

The irony of this would have been enjoyed by Frimmer, not that I intended confiding in him. He would have recognised that as his tethered goat I had no choices. It was so simple: if duty failed then self-preservation would succeed. Impatiently, I stirred custard round my jam sponge. Better concentrate on a straightforward task like feeding myself.

'You seem tired tonight,' said Mrs Gridley, presenting me with coffee.

'It has been a busy day. I was sent to Birmingham by my company. The trains and the buses do not seem to wait for each other.'

'They *ought* to provide a *car*,' she said, protectively.

'A long time since I have driven,' I said, slightly stressing my accent. I knew Madelaine was listening to me rather than to Albert. Mrs Gridley clucked a bit more, then distributed the rest of the coffee. Some of us retired into thought. Others did not.

'Come on, lad,' said Albert, bringing his coffee to my table, swinging a chair round and sitting facing me. 'You've not 'eard a single blind word I've been saying.'

'Sorry. I was thinking.' I had been on a tiny island in a lake in a park, staring into dark water, imagining her swimming under a boat.

Albert began a long story about an incredible sales scoop he was on the point of concluding. Something in my face discouraged him and the excitement in his voice died away. His shoulders slumped forward in acknowledgement of his lying. 'I was going to suggest a celebration drink,' he said, defensively. 'The ladies say they're not interested, but I thought you might be.'

'Yes, of course I am,' I said, heartily, surprising us both. 'Meet you in the hall about eight-thirty. The ladies are sure they will not come?'

'No thank you,' said Evelyn. 'I very rarely drink.'

'Please excuse me as well,' said Madelaine. 'I only arrived last night and really must finish unpacking and ironing. I hope you have a good time.'

'Thank you, my dear,' said Albert,

winking at me. 'You get yourself sorted out first and then we can all have some fun.'

I gulped my coffee and went to my room.

A few minutes later I heard my fellow-guests climbing the stairs together. Albert would be in the rear looking up skirts. Doors were shut. The house quietened. Downstairs, Mrs Gridley began the washing up, but only muffled echoes of her singing drifted to the first floor. She was pleased with life. Her rooms were full and her newest paying guest was a lady of some distinction. She had described herself to Mrs Gridley as a publisher's reader, and that sounded much more impressive than librarian or commercial traveller.

Mrs Gridley had passed on this information to me over tea, taken when Madelaine had left the house after her interview. Mrs Gridley did not know what a publisher's reader did but was not going to admit ignorance by asking. To me the description suggested a wide range of activities and irregular working hours. A publisher's reader might be difficult to keep under surveillance.

I knew where she was at that moment: one room removed from me, with Mrs Gridley's shocking pink room between us. But even living in the same house was no guarantee I would always know where she was. While Albert and I were out drinking she might decide to search my room. It was a waste of energy speculating how she might do that if I locked my door and there were other people in the house. They hadn't stopped *me* investigating and, with maybe fourteen murders to her credit, she was far more cunning than me.

When I went out I would leave my door ajar. I would be able to tell if anyone got in because my carpet was the right type for trapping visitors. No need for black threads, for items precariously balanced: tricks that might betray my true rôle and intentions.

At 8.30 I went downstairs to meet Albert in the hall.

'Hey-up,' he said. 'Whaddya need those for?' I was stuffing a pair of gloves into my jacket pocket. 'Summer's 'ere, you know.

Might not be as hot as Italy but it's not cold neither.'

'I need to give them wear,' I said. 'They are a present of my mother. When I see her again she will not be pleased if the gloves are still new. So I take them and get them used a little.'

'Aw, I see. Keep the old lady happy, eh? My motto too. Perhaps we ought to stay in and cheer up the lady guests. The dragon's just gone out to her Monday bingo.' 'Yes?' I said, trying to sound puzzled.

'You know. When the cat's — Oh, never mind. Come on.'

We got back about eleven o'clock. Albert, much the worse for wear, switched on the hall light and rushed into the downstairs lavatory next to Mrs Gridley's den. I started up the stairs alone. As I climbed out of the hall and into the dimness of the landing above, the staircase was transformed. The steps, rails, posts, even the carpet pattern, appeared to change into those in the entrance hall at West House. The state of my imagination was contradicted by the

156

precise care with which I drew on my new gloves. The soft rubber linings gripped clammily onto my damp palms.

The door of my room was ajar, apparently by the same amount as I had left it. Moonlight through the bedroom window cast the door edge shadow onto the wall, bisecting the light switch. I reached into the room past the door edge and, with gloved forefinger, switched on the light. I inspected the door carefully then pushed it open. As the soft glow of the centre light in my room seeped out onto the landing I looked across at the other bedroom doors: all tight shut. I knelt down, put my head close to the floor. The pile of my bedroom carpet, which I had carefully stroked with a comb before going out with Albert, showed the imprints of small pointed feminine shoes. They did not look like the prints of Evelyn's sensible brogues or Mrs Gridley's slippers.

Downstairs, Albert yanked on the lavatory chain, fired back the door-bolt and blundered along the hall. This was not a moment when I wanted to meet him. I edged round my door and looked into the room. It seemed safe enough. I shut myself in, locked the door, switched off the light. Precisely at that moment a cloud moved across the moon.

God, Albert was so slow! He struggled up the stairs, leaned on the post at the top. Then, hesitantly, he walked to my door. I held my breath. I could hear him muttering dispiritedly the other side of the door. The dark silence of my room decided him. He stumbled away to his own room. Thankfully, I switched on the centre light again but kept my back to the wall. That long wait in darkness had unnerved me. It had contained snakes under the bed. A board creaking was a trap-door opening; a curtain swaying was something seeping over the window sill into the room — a something that had extinguished the moon at the precise moment I had switched off the light. That the footprints on my carpet had been pointing out of the room as well as in had been no consolation. What had she left behind her? Perhaps the second attempt on my life was already set up. There was only one possibility of a domestic accident in my room.

I sat on the edge of the bed and looked at the bedside lamp which I had not switched on. The lamp stood on a scratched and battered bedside cabinet. The lamp column was coarse white china and supported a frilly pink shade on a metal frame. The lead from the wall-plug was also white and passed directly into the lamp base. From there, hidden from sight, it passed up the lamp column to the bulb. The bulb could be switched on by pressing a button just below it. There was also the usual arrangement of a switch at the wall-socket. Two switches. The wall-socket switch was already on. To light the lamp I had only to operate the button under the bulb which was under the shade with the metal frame. Metal frame.

Carefully, I switched off the wall-socket switch and pulled out the plug. There was no sign it had been tampered with. Holding the plug in my left hand I pressed in the lamp button switch with my right. I replaced the plug in the wall socket. All I had to do to complete the circuit was switch on the wall-switch. I could do that without putting a hand anywhere near the lamp itself. With right hand outstretched toward the wall-switch, I crouched against the wall as far away from the lamp as possible. A flicker of pain in my left knee reminded me it was only a week since that hit-and-run attempt. I depressed the switch. The bedside lamp lit up.

I sat on the floor and listened to my body working. Breathing was irregular. My bowels were in a shocking state that had nothing to do with the evening's drinking. I had known for some time that Madelaine Grey was to be stopped. Now I understood more clearly that she *had* to be. If I could not stop her with a solid weight of evidence I would have to do it in a more direct way.

I peeled off the clammy, rubber-lined gloves. My hands, mottled with pink blotches, were shaking slightly. When they were steady they were the hands of a marksman.

14

'Here, have a *hot* cup of coffee.' Mrs Gridley rubbed her left hip against the side of my chair. We were alone together in the dining-room.

'Thank you. It is my fault for coming late for breakfast.'

'Never *mind*, dear. At least you came down in a fit *state*.' She glared at Albert's dishevelled breakfast table. He had not been wished a good day when he left. 'Mind if I join you?' She dragged a chair, Madelaine's chair, across the carpet, slumped her heavy body next to mine and poured herself some coffee. She began to tell me how marvellous was summer, how hard it was not to be able to get away; how, self-sacrificingly, she would not leave us in the care of strangers while she took a holiday. Not that I was listening. It was Mrs Gridley's fate that the men in her life did not listen to her. Her husband had managed it by dying

161

young. Would that be my escape?

Earlier, I had watched Madelaine drive off in her noisy bright yellow car. Definitely not the hit-and-run car. Someone else's street-parked car is not difficult to borrow, to attempt an assault with, return to its parking place with doors relocked and only the mileometer reading to betray the theft. Who checks their mileometer reading in the morning to see if it has changed overnight? And as the assault had failed there would be no new marks on the bodywork. Madelaine had been thwarted by one thing: I could move faster than Corelli. Her ignorance of my identity was also the reason I knew my room had been searched. Corelli would not have laid the trap that caught her.

Now I had to search her room. Had to? Why jeopardise months of patient work? Truth was I could not live with the uncertainty of how next she would try to kill me.

'Are you all right, Mr Corelli?' Mrs Gridley laid her hand on my arm.

'Thank you. I have need of some fresh air. I will go to telephone my mother. I am not wanted at work until much later. Also I wonder if you will be kind — '

'Yes, dear?'

'Are you shopping this morning?'

'Yes, I am. Is there something I can get you?'

'Those tablets that Albert takes after drinking?'

'Oh — yes.' She smiled disapprovingly. 'I know what you want. I'll leave them on the hall table for you to pick up when you come in.'

I thanked her, escaped into the hall. Shutting the front door behind me I walked into the summer. By the time I arrived at the nearest telephone box I was warm again.

I dialled, waited, put the money in.

'Hello, Mother. Jake here.'

'You want to check?' The Duty Officer's voice was reassuringly calm.

'Suppose so.'

There was a loud click at his end of the line. I turned the handpiece around allowing it to sweep up and down all the walls and ceiling of the box. There was no one outside watching me, but I still felt stupid. A highly trained team, armed with the most sophisticated technology, was pitted against a lone madwoman. And how could she possibly have bugged a public call-box? Swearing to myself, I pointed the receiver at the telephone rest, then put it to my ear again.

'O.K.?' I asked.

'Yes. What can we do for you, Jack?'

'Where is she — Madelaine — at this moment?'

'Driving along the motorway toward the north-west. Could be aiming for Manchester or Liverpool.'

'Can you keep tabs on her all morning and ring The Larches number if she turns back toward Browcaister?'

'Can do. But you know the instructions. We have to keep our distance. The motorway police can monitor her progress but we're not closing in if she parks and starts walking. We'll observe in passing but not tail.'

'That'll do. It'll have to. But I need time in her room. I've already checked that Gridley is going shopping.'

'You got something?'

'Yes and no. She searched my room while I was out last night.'

'Sure?'

'Somebody bloody did! No reason to widen the field is there?'

'Er — no. Next move after searching her room?'

'Just waiting — and trying to give her another chance. Not much else I can do.'

'Suppose not.' There was a long silence. 'Right then, Jack. If she turns for home I'll ring your number, four rings then off. Then repeat.'

'Thanks. And you'll let me know what you can about how she spends her time today?'

'Yes, of course. Ring again tomorrow.'

Back at the house I answered Mrs Gridley's questions about my mother, and then told her I would be working in my room for the rest of the morning.

'What a pity I didn't know that before,' she said, coyly. 'I've arranged to meet Audrey for coffee when I've done the shopping. I could've come back here and shared it with you.'

'Not when it is my work time,' I said,

severely, as I climbed the stairs.

Sitting on the edge of my bed I watched my hands: steadier than they had been in the phone box. I undid my tie, stood up and draped it over the doorhook with my jacket, then I walked to the window. Downstairs, Mrs Gridley shrieked a goodbye through the banisters, opened and shut the front door, ground her feet into the gravel drive. I would allow her five minutes to discover if she had forgotten her purse or keys. Standing at my window, the sun burnishing me through the glass, I looked along the length of her back garden at unsullied lawn, decorously placed apple trees, newly painted white gate in the end wall. Beyond the wall was a back alley, other houses, other gardens. What the Gridley garden needed was a child's sandpit or a cheerful burrowing terrier.

I went downstairs into the hall. I put my hand on the front-door lock. Beyond the frosted glass no phantom shape materialised. I snapped the lock in place. Then I walked through the hall and into the immaculate kitchen. Mrs Gridley had remembered to lock the back door. Upstairs, I checked every room before I went to Madelaine's door. It was locked, but that was no trouble.

When I was sure no traps had been set, not even a combed carpet, I searched the room as my life depended on it. She had some lovely clothes, especially her underwear, and she preferred stockings to tights. Being made tumescent by these discoveries was just another kind of manipulation. I needed no reminders I was not in control.

In the bottom drawer of the dressing-table, beneath flame-coloured nightdresses, was a tool-kit in a smart leather case. Carefully, I removed each tool in turn and examined it. Every one showed some signs of wear. But was the kit any kind of clue? I looked at it as I had once, a child on a school outing to a dungeon, looked at a collection of torture implements. Their unpleasantness I had guessed at but had not been sure how any one of them might be applied on human flesh.

A woman needs a tool-kit for precisely the same reasons as a man: for those little attentions one's possessions demand, expecially one's car. But she did not keep the kit in her car. I sat back on my heels, inventoried the tools in the case. Some general purpose tools were missing, and the one small universal spanner would not be of much use in a car. But there were two screwdrivers, two pairs of pliers, a wire-stripper and a wire-clipper. The collection had something to say to me.

Even then I might not have heard had I not reacted so imaginatively (hysterically?) last night when I discovered she had got into my room. Electrician's tool-kit! The bedside lamp had not killed me, perhaps another fitting would. In so large a house there were over fifty points or fittings where incorrect wiring or a loose connection might cause a fatal accident. One thing saved me from having to check all those places: the fatal accident was to be mine. I was going to die either in my own bedroom, the dining-room, the lavatory or the bathroom. And any one of the last three rooms was only feasible as a killing ground if Madelaine could be sure of a time I, and no one else, would be there.

Very carefully, I put the tool-kit back into the bottom of the drawer, smoothed out the crackling silkiness (static electricity!) of her nightdresses, closed the drawer. Nothing else in her room spoke of any kind of death.

15

Perhaps Madelaine and I fell in love, although those particular words fit uncomfortably with events. Certainly, we were passionately interested in each other and, like lovers, each sought for any new fact or idea about the other. Sensually, we were very close. We shared the same lavatory where, following after her, I sat on the warm seat surrounded by her distinctive body smells. In the bathroom I lay in the tub that had so recently held her, my bathwater tainted with the sweeter fragrancies of her body. There were early morning greetings on the landing whilst in our dressing-gowns. There was coming home to each other every evening, eating the same meals and sleeping under the same roof; or lying sleepless under the same roof, each knowing the other was twenty feet away: a warm, slow-breathing, nearly naked body — alone.

I suppose more prosaic descriptions of our proximity might have applied equally to Albert, Evelyn and Mrs Gridley. But I no more cared for Evelyn than Madelaine cared for Albert. And as for Albert caring for Evelyn: that was outside my field of vision. If something did not relate directly to the axis passing through Madelaine and myself it was lost in superspace. With Mrs Gridley it was slightly different. I knew she had her rheumy eye on me and, in spite of her personal seediness, I was forming a kind of sympathetic attachment for her — but no more than that. Perhaps it had to do with my foreknowledge that some sort of terror was soon to inhabit her house.

Mrs Gridley was also involved in terms of geography: she slept in the room that separated Madelaine and me. As I lay sweating on my bed I had to remind myself that the creaking bedspring, the soft nightsigh came from her and not from Madelaine. Thus reminded, I focused even harder on Madelaine. My erotic thoughts were stimulated by recollection of holding her naked at my feet.

In one respect our relationship was stronger, more intense than being in love: I mean in its excitement. We were locked together in events the outcome of which was not to be that she took my penis into her vagina, but that she took my life before I could take hers. (In the turmoil of being with her there was no longer a place in my thinking for the more mundane outcome of arresting her.)

That I was also afraid was obvious enough, but it was part of that excitement, part of the challenge. Being afraid for myself was somehow all muddled up with being afraid for her. I never worked out the distinction between those two, although I recognised that fear for the loved one is partly a projection of the fear for one's own safety. Maybe love and fear are different expressions of the same thing. Certainly, I was blinded by one or the other.

Later, and much too late, I was able to identify the area of my blindness. Almost literally entranced by her proximity and by the intensity of our relationship, I had wrongly chosen to regard her as cunning rather than crazy, resourceful rather than demented. My single-eyed colleagues must have realised I was becoming blind to her madness but they lacked either the will or the words to challenge me. I suppose Frimmer tried the next time I phoned H.Q. Once I had cleared myself and the phone-box with the Duty Officer he came on the line. He was brisk, but that did not conceal his anxiety.

'I feel you're very exposed there, Bull. Is there any way you can think of for us to get back-up in a bit closer?'

'Not without frightening her off.'

'Are you still quite sure about electronic surveillance?'

'Yes, sir. In the first place that sort of evidence is very dicey in court, nearly as dicey as D.S. Douglas saying he *thought* she was the driver of the hit-and-run car. Secondly, more important, she's sharp enough to spot what might be set up. That'd bring the whole thing down round our heads. She'd simply back off. All our work would be wasted.'

There was a long pause, then Frimmer asked: 'Any specific ideas about another attack on you?'

'Yes, sir. Could be electrocution. She's got a tool-kit that would suit. And the possibility relates to several other deaths on our list.'

'That's right!' Frimmer was suddenly very emphatic. 'That's right! And it might relate to some information I've got for you. One of the items Grey purchased in Manchester was an electric fire.'

'Christ!' I implored, seeing myself in the bath, a corpse under water, electric fire still hissing in my groin. 'But hang on, sir. How d'you know that?'

'Don't flap, Bull. We didn't actually tail, but when one of our lads checked back in the department store she had visited the staff remembered her for that purchase. They thought it odd someone should buy a fire in the middle of a heat wave. She bought other goods, but assistants in other departments either could not recall her or couldn't remember details of what she bought.'

The conversation really died then but

we pushed it around for a few more minutes before I rang off. I had identified the concern in Frimmer's voice, but all *that* did for me was make me angrier. There's none so deaf —

A different kind of concern was expressed by Una and Kathy during my next visit. They had begun to relax with me, partly because I had become a regular client who behaved himself and paid well. By mutual consent we had settled into a comfortable arrangement whereby I bought them for a whole afternoon. That we remained active all afternoon was usually a tribute to their skills rather than my appetite. That week it was different, and the girls giggled over possible explanations of my randiness. They put me to the test with some strenuous threeplay (and foreplay) in, over and across an armchair laid on its back. By the time we finished up in their giant bed, drinking gin and eating slabs of fruit-cake, I had been worked out in several senses. To make sure I was entirely satisfied, Una started an interesting hunt for cake crumbs.

When I left at 5.30 their sheer animal warmth and vitality had exhausted me physically but had also poulticed my emotions. Their taking and giving was characterised by simplicity. I paid: they gave value. Because I was healthy, straight and fully sexed they also gave a bonus in kind. If Frimmer had met me then it is just possible he would have understood why I insisted on jeopardising our work in that particular way.

As I staggered happily down the stairs and out onto the pathway, Una leaned out of the front window of their first floor flat and called to me: 'Don't forget it's Thursday next week, Jake.' Enjoying her indiscretion, I smiled back at her and waved.

I turned into the main road, and her words took on a different, more depressing meaning. Would I live that long? By the time I reached my room my mood was very different from what it had been while licking crumbs off Una's thighs. I wedged my door shut, using the wedge I had carved from scrapwood found in a gutter. I lay on the bed and thought of all

176

the deaths that might not require the opening of a door. Under the floor were gas-pipes. Electricity was already in the room, in the walls, in the ceiling. I was reminded of a Thurber story about electricity and began to laugh out loud. The silence that followed laughter was broken by something like a whimper.

16

Friday lunchtime in the King's Head, enjoying whisky, home-made pâté and hot toast, I saw Kathy working her trade. She caught sight of me just after she had snared a pimply, stout, elderly business-man. I grimaced at her client's back, gave a thumbs down, to which she replied with two fingers while helping him on with his coat. What sort of man wears a topcoat in such hot weather? What sort of man was I to share Kathy with him? I ordered another drink.

Later, I walked slowly to the little walled garden next to the town hall. For an hour on a fine afternoon, sitting shirt-sleeved in the sun, I could think of it as my garden. Only the three meths men on the other bench might have disputed title with me, but they were in most senses incapable. I enjoyed their distant company partly because their occupation of the only other seat discouraged anyone else from lingering.

The garden was about half an acre enclosed by high brick and stone walls mantled with ancient climbing plants not known to me. Between the walls and the brick paths parallel to them lay burgeoning, full-stocked herbaceous borders which, within the suntrap of the walls, were at least a fortnight ahead of the summer. In the centre of the garden, separated from the borders by the paths, lay the rose-beds; my kind of rose-beds in which each bush almost touched its neighbours. At opposite ends of the garden the paths widened to accommodate the two wooden seats that faced each other across the roses. I had the north seat facing the sun, the meths men had the south seat in the shade of the south wall. The drink made them sweat enough.

There was only one entrance to the garden: an iron gate set in an arch in the west wall. To reach it from the High Street one had to walk down a long, dismal, vomit-stained alley between office blocks and the backs of shops; perhaps another reason for being left in peace. I supposed a garden surrounded by high walls and with only one gateway constituted a trap. But I was not troubled by that, not even when, looking up through sun-dazzled eyes, I realised the measured footsteps were Madelaine's.

I lifted my briefcase off the bench, and she sat beside me, gave a sigh of relief as she put her full shopping-bag on the ground.

'Hello,' she said. 'What are you doing here? No work?'

'No,' I said. 'But why is it you also do not work?'

'Being a publisher's reader I can plan my own work-time,' she said simply, as if that explained our meeting.

'Oh yes. Lovely day.'

'It is, Jake. And they say the whole week-end will be fine,' she said, uncharacteristically running a hand through her hair.

'Yes.'

'What are your plans for the week-end?'

'Er — I do not know.'

'Would you like it if we spend some

time together? We could go to the boating-lake tomorrow, or swimming perhaps. Do you swim?'

'Not very well,' I lied, gasping slightly as if from the heat. Not even she was that bold? Was she?

She proposed the time, the places, her car to take us from our digs to the boating-lake and the pool. I agreed, thanked, blinked in the sunlight. The sweat patches under her arms, staining her summer frock, were spreading, enlarging.

'You have never seen this garden before?' I asked.

'No. This is my first visit. I saw it marked on the town plan. It's lovely here. Listen to the bees.'

We listened while I thought about the coincidence of her first visit taking place when I was in the garden.

'Other ways it is quiet,' I said. '*They* do not talk. Once they sang.' I pointed at the three sleeping drunks. She laughed, said she hoped they sang in tune.

Ten minutes later we were walking out of the garden toward the car park. I carried my briefcase and her shopping-bag. She drove us back to The Larches where Mrs Gridley was put out by our arrival together. But the sun had also unhinged her and we were invited into the back garden for afternoon tea. I sat there with my women while the week-end settled round us.

Saturday, Madelaine and I swam, boated, sunbathed and read, accompanied by most of the population of Browcaister. Evening found us at a riverside pub drinking iced lager. Outwardly, we were a sunburnt couple who had enjoyed the day together and were perhaps prospecting for the night as well. I suspected that inwardly she was like me: a mass of raw nerve-endings that owed little to the fierce inflammation of the sun.

Later, in one unguarded moment, when meeting her outside the pub after visiting the lavatories, I saw a troubled expression on her face: perhaps a mixture of anger and bewilderment. It was the look of a small child who throws a ball to a friend only to see that so-called friend run off with it instead of throwing it back. I believe she was disoriented by feelings that drew her toward me instead of repelling. Unlike poles attract.

Pleading tiredness and too much sun, she drove us back early to the house. We hardly spoke. Maybe we had established some kind of nervously exhausted stalemate. On the landing she proposed we toss a coin for first bath. I explained I always preferred a late bath because it helped me to sleep. She smiled then made some joke about me being the phantom late night bather Mrs Gridley was after. Then, like a bird in its swerving flight, her right hand brushed my left cheek.

Behind my locked door, lying on the bed, I listened to the muffled sounds of her movements in the bath. Sleepily, I travelled back into the day, to the moments of her shy smile at my unspoken appreciation of her lithe beauty; to the moments of touching which, however accidental, made the heart lurch. And how I had enjoyed the furtive appreciative glances of other men watching her straight suppleness, the vitality that shone in her; in her balanced walk, as in black swimsuit with red swimming-cap in hand, she made her way along the poolside. And later, in her summer-flowered dress, stepping coltlike into the unstable, rocking rowing boat.

Enjoying sensuous recollections while drowsing face down on my bed, my shirt bitter-sweetly brushing my newly sun-burned back, was pleasurable enough. But it was made possible not just by the passing day but also by the security of a locked and wedged door. Later, I woke in darkness, cold and cramp-ridden on the bed.

I looked at my watch. If I was quick I could steal a bath and be back in my room before Albert came roaring in from his Saturday night drinking, and Mrs Gridley came back from Bingo grousing at her luck. I collected a fresh, dry towel, soap and flannel, my damp swimming things and my keys. Very quietly, determined not to disturb Madelaine, I left my room, locked the door behind me and walked to the bathroom next door. It was empty, the bath now cold to my touch, but I could still smell the trace of her talcum powder. Her damp swimsuit was hanging from the line over the bath. Coyly, I pegged my trunks next to it. As I draped my towels over the heated rail I caught sight of myself in the mirror. I inspected my hairline, checking to see if I needed to redye to maintain that Italian blackness. Not yet.

17

Adherent to the customs of her trade, Mrs Gridley allowed Sunday breakfast to begin and end half an hour later than on weekdays. Having overslept, I came last into the dining room. Albert was in no state to reply to my good morning, Evelyn nodded and grunted in her lumpy way, Madelaine smiled and sent back her good morning like a song. As I sat down at my table I was uncomfortably aware of the sharp look Evelyn was turning on us. I think Madelaine was also aware, judging by the care with which she dissected her sausage. Evelyn snorted into her teacup. It occurred to me that our Evelyn had the power to introduce additional complications into an already complex situation. I also concentrated on sausages.

When I stood up to leave the dining room, Madelaine and Evelyn rolled their napkins, pushed back their chairs. I walked toward the door. Moving surprisingly quickly, Evelyn neatly stepped between Madelaine and myself and followed me into the hall.

'Saw an old friend of ours, yesterday,' said Evelyn, spitefully.

'Yes?' I said.

Madelaine walked past us and began to climb the stairs. Evelyn and I watched her. Then Evelyn spoke again, more loudly, as though determined Madelaine should overhear.

'Yes. Frederick Robinson. I bumped into him, quite by accident of course.'

'Oh, he is well?' I was praying Madelaine would be out of range of our voices.

'No, not very. But then he never is, is he?'

'No,' I said, after a pause. Madelaine was at the top of the stairs, turning toward her room.

'He's expecially sad you haven't contacted him, Jake.'

I knew that if she mentioned my lies about getting Robinson a job in my firm and Madelaine heard — . Attack is the best defence.

'But, Evelyn, *you* are the one he misses. I am sure of it. Before he left here — ' I paused again.

'What did he say?' Her eyes glittered. Madelaine was forgotten.

'He said he would miss you. He knows you to be a very fine lady.' This appalling lie, appalling in more than one sense, was uttered as Madelaine shut her bedroom door. Relief spurred me on. 'I think he wished to make me jealous.'

'Oh,' said Evelyn, breathlessly.

'Good morning,' I said, and ran up the stairs. As I unlocked my door Madelaine came out of her room carrying her rolled towel and costume, her reading-glasses and a bag of books. We hesitated. But yesterday had given us both sufficient to think about.

'I'll see you tonight,' she said, smiling.

'Yes,' I said. 'Have another lovely day.'

'Thank you.' She blushed slightly as she walked past me to the stairs. I watched the shining brown crown of her head sink down the staircase, leaving me tethered in my very small clearing.

I spent the morning dithering in my

room. I supposed I could have gone out, but instead I chose to pretend I was afraid of meeting Madelaine. There was some truth in this because an accidental meeting might be interpreted as intentional. My colleagues were being so careful not to tail her I dared not risk creating the impression that I was.

Mrs Gridley saved my day, or at least saved my afternoon, by announcing rather grandly at lunch that in view of the continuing fine weather she was placing her back garden at our disposal for the rest of the day. Evelyn looked warily at Albert and me. He was busy explaining to me why he had not won a fortune on the Australian football pools yesterday, and I was pretending I cared. Encouraged by our indifference Evelyn later appeared in the garden wearing a purple suntop and rather too tight tennis shorts. The only obvious effect of this display was that Albert, who was lying in a deckchair under one of the apple trees, pulled his old panama hat down over his face. I continued oiling my body. Mrs Gridley continued to rattle her washing up at the kitchen sink.

So the day slipped away with the four of us performing together those little social arabesques that characterise English boarding-house life: the interlocking patterns of pretended and real indifferences, of slightly overstressed politenesses, the occasional mildly reproving conversations. No doubt Mrs Gridley would be telling her friend Audrey of her own thoughtfulness and generosity, of 'poor Evelyn's' ill-fitting garb, of my Italian self-expression, ('Only wearing his swimming trunks, my dear. And such funny marks on his body!'), and of Albert's slow recovery from the excesses of Saturday night. And, of course, there would be references to her own social graces in the way she presided over the tea tray.

Madelaine did not return to the house until after dark when we were all in our rooms. As I pulled the single sheet across my body, hoping to sleep as well as last night, I knew there was no need to worry about finding out where Madelaine had been. Someone was going to tell me. Although she was not tailed she was observed in passing by any policeman she drove near. I wondered what she would have said had she known that the registration number of her little yellow car was engraved in the mind of every policeman in the country. And I wondered what they would have said if they had known why.

Our new working week fell into the familiar pattern except that my casual encounters with Madelaine were now closely observed by Evelyn. No need to bother with wearisome speculations about what was going on in *that* head. In mine were expressions of feelings that we were all approaching some climax. However casually and calmly Madelaine and I met and talked neither of us could pretend that Saturday had not happened, had not shifted and distorted the magnetic field that held us. For me, denying Saturday was as ridiculous as denying the hit-and-run attempt, the body in the lake, the cabinets bulging with the files of analyses of strange lives and stranger deaths. But most of all my mind lived with, racked itself with, the assumption that the approaching climax concerned my own death. I even got that wrong.

As the week passed I felt Madelaine and I drew closer at each meeting. Morning greeting seemed to express something like regret that we had spent another night apart. And the evening conversations implied that the approaching night might also be shared. I *knew* all this was not taking place inside my head. Evelyn's watchfulness confirmed the reality of what I believed was happening, as did Mrs Gridley's increasingly frosty attitude toward Madelaine. Only Albert appeared unaware of all the subtle and not so subtle undercurrents swirling round us. His week had already been blighted by Monday evening. Beside his dinner mat he had found a letter delivered that morning after he had left for work: an unequivocal message from an ex-wife's solicitor.

'Don't ever do the daft thing and marry,' he said to me mournfully. I shook my head and watched him dribble soup down his Old Etonian tie. The nearest he had ever been to Eton was a primary school outing to Windsor. 'Sex is all right, I suppose,' he conceded, grudgingly. 'But marriage don't do it good.'

Having sex very much on my own mind made me sympathetic toward Albert, but I did not dwell for long on his difficulties.

The unremitting titillation of my sexuality that Madelaine personified made me even more impatient than usual for Thursday afternoon with Kathy and Una. Strangely, my randiness was further excited by Evelyn's malicious interest in every word and gesture that linked me with Madelaine. As I skipped — well, nearly skipped — to the girls' flat after lunch on Thursday I enjoyed the teasing idea that my two little tarts were unwittingly substitutes for Madelaine and Evelyn. Chuckling coarsely to myself, I pushed against the front door which the girls had left ajar. It would not open any further, was stuck against something. I pushed harder, and the door moved back enough for me to squeeze through the gap. As I did so I was aware of a disgusting smell.

The blood-smeared door was jammed against Kathy's head. The first slashing cut had gouged out her left eye and then grated into the bone of her nose. As she had staggered under that blow her dressing-gown must have fallen open. Unhindered, the second even fiercer blow had entered her naked body just above her pink-dyed pubic hair and disembowelled her. In falling, already a gutted corpse, Kathy had twisted over onto her back with her head against the door. Some very small part of my mind debated with itself the unlikelihood of this. Her intestines, the yards of them that the books tell us, had spilled out of her and were settling greasily against the skirting-boards on each side of the hall. And all her black and black-red blood at my feet. In death a small neat compact woman had become hideously large.

If she had screamed at the first slashing blow then Una — I made to step forward, but there was no room past Kathy. Nor was there any need. As I looked up the stairs leading to their flat I saw a limp hand protruding between the banisters of the second flight. And the deep red stair carpet was turning black; a blackness creeping round the corner of the stairs and slowly down the lower flight to the hall, toward what had been Kathy. In order to reach Una the killer must have trodden in Kathy. With the most appalling heaving motion I vomited into the poor dead face, into the red mouth which, only days ago, had held my sex.

I remember nothing else until I discovered I was sitting on that sunny bench in 'my' garden, my mind struggling with another horror. In getting out, the killer must not only have trodden in Kathy again but must also have stooped to drag the slit body bag closer to the door. Then, as the killer backed out, Kathy's head fell against the door to hold it almost shut. The killer had not wanted the bodies seen by a passer-by, nor had she wanted me warned off by finding the door jammed tight shut and receiving no reply to my ringing. I had found the bodies in exactly the way she had planned.

She.

I never doubted it was she. I never doubted I had led her there and that she had been near enough to hear of my arrangements for the meeting.

Later, I heard the distant, then closer, then receding anxious cry of ambulances. So, someone had found my girls. I did not wonder who, only whether they had been as sick as me.

When Jim Douglas came into the garden I did not immediately recognise him. Then he made a helpless shrugging gesture with his shoulders, and I knew him. He sat beside me on my left. After a little while he put his hand under my elbow and helped me stand up.

18

'You will not kill her,' said Frimmer, irritably, for the second time. I did not reply. The room was silent again.

Fear made the uniformed superintendent restive. Fidgeting on his chair he stubbed his foot on a tin can and sent it clattering across the stone floor. Embarrassed, he fiddled with his gloves and hat. In the emaciating light of the one small bulb in a cracked plastic shade, his uniform badges glinted dully; just enough for me to be sure he was there, badgerlike in his dark corner. Whenever I looked at him he looked away from me. Perhaps if we had been on his home ground he could have managed a bit better, but Frimmer had taken care of that.

I supposed I had been brought to a 'safe' house. The window, which had once looked onto the basement area and the flight of worn stone steps down which Jim had helped me, was boarded over. There was no furniture in the room other than the two chairs. I had one, the Super the other. The grate was heaped with cold grey ashes and part scorched, rusting metal cans. Peeling wallpaper lingered on the mouldering walls, and the ceiling was a sagging mosaic of cracked damp plaster. It was a room summer never reached. In winter it might be a hibernation for tramps. Now it was a refuge for nervous coppers.

The door behind me was opened and shut. Whoever entered the room stood behind me. I did not turn round.

'Well?' Frimmer said, as if casting a flat stone onto water.

'The killer was wearing protective clothing. That explains the peculiar smear marks in the blood on the inside of the front door.' I did not know the voice.

'She's still got to get rid of it,' said Frimmer.

'Tail?' That sounded like Jim.

'No,' said Frimmer. 'Stay as we are.'

'That's why they're dead,' I shouted. We were all startled, expecially me. 'If you had the sense to bloody well tail her those girls — '

'Shut up,' hissed Frimmer, stepping close, bending down so his eyes were level with mine. 'You dishonest little bastard! They died for one reason only: you did not obey my orders and keep away from them. The responsibility is entirely yours.'

The superintendent shrugged again. Someone must have told him that was not the way to speak to a sick man. Behind me, others stood still, perhaps ready to spring at me if I lashed out at Frimmer. I could not have raised a hand.

'You know precisely the why and how we've been watching her,' said Frimmer. (Funny how none of us could speak her name.) 'We've always known her general location, and that's been as close as we've dared get. Today, she did what she quite often does: left her car in the Castle Museum car park all day and took her work into the reading-room.' I knew all about that pattern, had more than once smiled at the fact of she and I in different reading-rooms: separate yet linked. Today that pattern had been erased. 'Well,' continued Frimmer, heavily, 'she set off to the swimming pool about an hour later. Local bobby spotted her going in. The next sighting was — was after the murders, about two hours after. She was seen driving her car out of the Museum car park.'

'Unmarked?' I asked. Frimmer knew I didn't mean the car.

'Yes. The Super here's got all his men looking for a bloodstained bundle of clothing and some kind of large carving knife. Nothing so far.'

The door creaked open once again. A written message was held near my right shoulder, taken by Frimmer, passed on to the superintendent. He held it obliquely toward the light so he could read it: gesture of an old man.

'Our Forensic say D.S. Bull is in the clear, sir,' he said to Frimmer.

'So Bull stays on this case.'

'No, sir.' The superintendent hesitated, then ploughed on. 'This is our patch you're working on and we've got responsibilities which — '

'Nonsense!' said Frimmer. 'You and I

have exactly the same responsibilities, exactly the same objectives. Don't start trying to flannel me just because local pride's been hurt. You stay with previous instructions for observing and monitoring. I'll take care of the close-in work.'

'Sorry, sir,' said the superintendent, standing up, flicking the seat of his trousers with his gloves. 'You taking care has led to a double murder in my town. I can't accept that you are as much in control as you say.' The silence that followed was not describable. The unfortunate officer began to pick at the buttons of his jacket and shuffle his feet. Frimmer let the silence ride on. Eventually:

'Good afternoon, Superintendent,' said Frimmer, quietly. Head down, the man left the room.

'Now, young Bull,' growled Frimmer, 'you open your ears wide!' He nodded at someone behind me. Jim Douglas stepped into view carrying a radio transceiver. 'Your life might depend on hearing this next bit. Understand me, Bull?'

'Yes, sir.'

'You have to go back in there, agreed?'

'Sir. Is she back at the house?'

'Just arrived. Cool as you like. She is the *most* dangerous — ' He hesitated. 'You know that for yourself!' We all thought about what I knew. Then Frimmer pointed at the transceiver Jim was holding. 'You take that. No argument. You'll just have to hide it in your room somewhere. I'm ordering you to take that chance of blowing the case. We're now far beyond the point of leaving you entirely alone. The set has been modified so that if we want to contact you, or you us, a red light can be set to come on. Show him, Douglas.' Our three faces were suddenly struck with a blood light, tart's light. (Too late to save *them*.) Jim switched it off.

'If you are O.K., Jack,' said Jim, 'you just press this button next to the light and the lights your end and our end go out for two hours. Got it?' I nodded. 'It's also an ordinary radio so if we want to call you up we can. But the light means we can check your safety without anyone breaking silence.' I nodded again.

'There's another refinement,' said Frimmer. 'You can set that red light device for periods of less than two hours, using that dial there.'

'Continuously if necessary,' interrupted Jim.

'Yes — continuously,' said Frimmer, more sharply.

I didn't say anything. I wondered what would be happening to me if I needed to set the contact light on continuous.

'Well,' said Frimmer. 'I think we can start to get you back in. Your story is that you saw a terrible road accident and helped the police with enquiries. You can't discuss details because it upset you too much — you hysterical Italian you. Got that? Our killer will know exactly what you saw but we've no idea how she'll use that knowledge. No idea how to prove she did it either. We're operating on yet another unsupported assumption. If she did butcher them perhaps she hoped you'd be charged with the murders.'

'Don't sound right,' I said. 'Somehow not sick *enough*.'

'With you, Jack. More likely it's

something to do with putting down tarts as she puts down rapists.'

'No hope of nailing her?'

'Remote. Another motiveless, random killing. No clues found so far, and she was not seen in that locality. The only thing we *know* is that if she did it she got bloodstained. Hence the interest in protective clothing as well as the murder weapon. I've a nasty feeling she's been far too quick for us to find them in circumstances that might lead back to her.

'Now then, getting you back in starts with you telephoning Mrs Gridley to say you've witnessed an accident and will be back late for dinner.'

Once again Jim Douglas appeared beside me, this time holding a telephone. 'We're wired in,' he said. 'I'll dial for you.'

I spoke to Mrs Gridley, apologised, explained, cut short her queries, rang off.

'Feeling all right?' asked Jim. I shook my head. 'I'll take the phone away,' he said, embarrassed. As he left the room Mr Stone entered. He came and stood in front of me. I did not stand up.

'Can you manage this?' he asked.

'Yes, sir. Think so.' I knew what he meant.

'I appreciate the strain — '

'Not just today you know, sir.'

'I understand,' said Stone. 'You remember my lecture: The Murder Triangle?'

'Sir?'

'How the triangle of detective, victim and killer so often works?'

'Detective gets to know killer by getting to know victim.'

'Right, Jack. Now this case — you are detective and victim. You understand what I'm saying to you?'

'I think so.' I was also understanding that his lapse into schoolmasterish behaviour was a result of intense embarrassment. Perhaps he was preparing me for more bad news.

'It is,' he went on, doggedly, 'simply that, being at two corners of the triangle at the same time, you are inevitably under tremendous pressure. That's what I meant.'

'Er — yes. You're wondering if my

mind is up to it?'

'Yes.' Strangely enough the bluntness of his answer gave me a feeling of warmth. His openness was so much a contrast with everything else that was going on. Perhaps it also said something about our mutual respect.

'I'm O.K., sir. Need a night's rest, time to collect my wits. Never felt so angry, you know.'

'Pity,' snapped Frimmer, apparently bored by expressions of concern. 'You stay angry and you'll get dead.'

19

I recollected I had sat in my garden again, then had walked back to The Larches. Something about uniformed foot patrols always in the distant view. Guarding? Mrs Gridley had been kind; had offered late dinner which I could not have kept down. I had accepted her whisky.

'Where is everybody else?' I had asked.

'*They* are all out,' Mrs Gridley had said. 'Went out together about ten minutes before you came in. They asked *me*, of course, but my place is here, *especially* being worried about you.'

'I am most sorry you missed — '

'Nothing to miss. Mr Hammond talked some nonsense about his job, something about a *celebration*, persuaded the two ladies to go with him. They had planned to wait for *you*, but I told 'em you'd phoned saying you'd be late. Didn't tell 'em why,' she had added, laying a hand on my arm. 'It can be *our* secret if you like.'

'It is a strange thing,' I had said, carefully, 'the two ladies to go with Albert. It has not happened before.'

'No accounting for *taste*, dear. Some of us have it, some of us don't.'

'Yes. Er — I must go to the bath now.' I had handed her the empty glass.

I had showered and bathed and showered and — . But when I was clean it had made no difference to the stench of Kathy.

Later, I had overheard some conversation, an argument between women. Now, it escaped me. Fully awake, I listened. There was no disagreeable sound. Above me the roof tiles clicked with the expansiveness of morning. Beyond my sunstained curtains birds sang. Downstairs, Mrs Gridley sang along with her radio. When the disc jockey spoke I recognised the cracked elderly voice. I picked up my watch. 10.15.

I swung my feet to the floor, stood up, quickly sat down again. While waiting for my head I looked round the room. *Bars* do not a prison — . Then I was looking at the wedge under the door. Something wrong. My head cleared even as I snatched my feet up from the floor and onto the bed. Rolling sideways, I lowered my head over the edge of the bed, looked under it. No snakes. A harmless pair of slippers — mine; a few wisps of dust — awaiting Mrs Gridley's eagle eye. Nothing else.

I got off the bed, searched the room. Nothing touched. The radio was under my clean shirts. The red light was on. I prodded the button and the light went out. No one wanted to speak with me.

I walked to the door and pushed against it. With a loud click the catch engaged. However unwell I had been I would not have left the door like that. Now I was sure about the wedge. I managed to pull it clear. Across its upper surface was the fresh, clear imprint of the bottom edge of the door. On the door was a small crush mark in the paint. Someone had tried to get to me without realising the door was wedged. Thoughtfully, I slid the wedge back in place. There was something else not explained.

I washed and dressed, went downstairs.

Mrs Gridley met me in the hall.

'Heard you moving about, dear. How are you?'

'I am well, thank you.' I doubted if the son of an Italian immigrant would know the expression: 'mouth like a birdcage'.

'Would you like some coffee, my dear?'

'Yes, please.'

'Come into the den. It's all ready.'

It was, so was buttered toast and marmalade. Her dead husband watched me from the photoframe. The ducks still bombed. They would have recognised my mouth. I skirted the settee, sat in the armchair. But there was something more immediate than romance on the widow's mind.

'I hope you weren't disturbed early this morning, Mr Corelli.'

'No. A police doctor gave me a medicine to help me to sleep.'

'That's good.' She hesitated for a moment, but the bond which she fantasised as linking us was too strong. She had to share. 'Only before breakfast, quite *early*, I was in the hall and heard a funny noise on the landing. I went up there and found that Miss Hutchinson trying to get into *your* room.'

'Oh,' I said. Now I knew not only the intruder, and who had disturbed her, but also why that catch had been left so revealingly disengaged. 'Disturbed while entering'.

'Miss Hutchinson — your Madelaine! — ' (I laid back my ears, the possessive sounded ominous) — 'she *said* she was worried about how you were. She would be — wearing that *silly* nightie. Belongs on a young kid. And, of course, she didn't think about bumping into Mr Hammond on his way to the *bathroom*. I told her straight, I did, there on the landing. This is a nice *respectable* guest-house and I mean to keep it that way. Can't blame me can you? This is my home as well as my living you know.'

'Er — yes. But how could a person get into another room?'

'People leave the catch off the door. They forget you know.' She looked thoughtfully at the photos on the cabinet. 'I suppose it's a compliment in a way. People feel at home.' Then with a sudden burst of energy, and almost tearfully: 'But *that* woman's not going to spoil things. She'll have to go. Bad enough last *night* — all that noise and fuss.'

'Oh.'

'Yes, well. I mean. They came back from the pub, not that I've anything against drink as you know, but enough's enough. *She* was — er — a bit silly — if you know what I mean. That fool Hammond was too far gone to notice. He just kept telling her she was lovely. Evelyn was quite *disgusted* by the pair of them. Told me she *definitely* wouldn't be going out with *them* again.'

'I missed all the bother.'

'Just as well. But I don't mind telling you, dear, if there's any more of her nonsense, she'll have to *go*. Miss Hutchinson, I mean.'

'Ah.' That was all I could say. Was Madelaine risking everything she had set up by trying to enter my room when other people were about?

Carefully, I spread the glistening marmalade over the buttered toast, evenly, evenly; sliding it into the crusty corners. Mrs Gridley sat silent watching my skill and control, while everywhere else, everything else, everyone else slammed uncontrolled into each other and into me.

'See Browcaister's made the papers,' said Mrs Gridley, pulling a folded newspaper from under the cushions of the settee. 'There. I've marked it. Very nasty!' She pushed it at me like a customs officer showing me the unrecognisable passport photo of myself.

BRUTAL MURDER OF TWO WOMEN

'Yes,' I said, dry-mouthed, reading.

The paper, still warm from Mrs Gridley's bum, contained a simple, half-correct account; no mention of how they smelt in death. They were discovered by a gypsy woman selling lucky charms. She had found the door open and looked in. Taken to hospital suffering from shock. She, I thought, will give up lucky charms for a while. Police inquiries etc. etc. But I had to face the question Mrs Gridley was asking but not uttering.

'It is horrible,' I said. 'The accident I

saw was bad enough, but it was accident, not deliberate.'

'Oh,' she said, half-relieved, half-disappointed. 'Mind you, says they were *prostitutes*. Never know who'll be on their doorstep, do they?' She looked at me again from under those quizzing ginger eyebrows. But this time the question contained no threat.

'I do not understand such women,' I said, primly, tossing the paper onto the settee beside her. 'They disgust. I hope never to meet one.'

'Ah,' she said, apparently convinced of something. 'Would you like me to make you some more fresh coffee, my dear?'

When I escaped, without cutting her throat, I walked into town and went to the riverside pub where Madelaine and I had been last week-end.

'Two deaths ago.' The barman dropped my change onto the bar and backed away. I had not meant to speak. I took my double whisky into the garden, sat on the grass and watched the boaters on the river. Beside me lay my jacket, the radio in a side pocket. Nobody wanted to speak to me. Later, I walked back through the town to The Larches. It seemed important to be in my room before the other lodgers came in from their work. I skulked there listening to the sounds of their return. My unsettled bowels began pinching me as dinner time approached, and the pain had nothing to do with hunger.

Mrs Gridley played the gong. I listened to the other three go downstairs. Then, taking a deep breath, I plunged out of the room, down the stairs and into my seat in the dining room. The three of them sat staring at me. Mrs Gridley had blabbed after all.

Evelyn and Albert offered good evening and sympathetic glances before looking down at their place-mats. But *she* smiled; smiled and said her 'hello'.

That smile was a kind of turning point, something like a gift. It confirmed her guilt and also the certainty of my survival. I could not explain that. Within me a lot of self-defeating anxieties began to wither away leaving me with a sense of identity regained. I couldn't explain that either.

But she still had cards of her own to play.

We sat, the four of us, at our separate tables drinking coffee. No one suggested moving to the residents' lounge. Albert tried to pump me about the accident, but Evelyn cut him short by expressing the hope that I felt recovered from the shock. I said that I did but needed another early night.

'I think we all do,' said Madelaine, abruptly. 'But for different reasons.'

'Aye,' said Albert, reluctantly accepting my refusal to gossip about the accident. 'We 'ad a good party last night. Sorry you missed it, Jake.'

'Yes,' I said, 'so am I sorry.' My accent sounded worse than ever to me.

'Well, lad — we can always arrange another.'

'Er — yes, thank you, Albert. But now I go to my room.'

I locked and wedged my door, checked the radio, dozed on the bed.

At 10.30 p.m. I woke from foul dreams. I was soaked in sweat, decided to have a bath. I stripped naked, put on my dressing-gown, grabbed my bag and towel, scurried to the bathroom, locking my room door behind me. After a cool bath I dried off and returned to my room.

As I put the key in the lock other doors opened. I turned, stood transfixed, as Madelaine advanced on me. She was still wearing the high-necked black dress worn at dinner. Above the black only the eyes lived in the white face. She stopped in front of me. We stood silent, twelve inches apart. Eventually, her face cracked into the same smile it had worn in the dining room.

'Feeling good, Jake?' she said. She slipped her right hand into the front of my dressing-gown, grasped my penis. 'Not a lot of life there, either,' she said, still smiling her sick smile.

The disgusted, sudden indrawn breath taken by Evelyn shattered the moment. We both turned our heads, watched Evelyn backing into her room. Madelaine released her hold on my unresponsive organ, then stepped back as I began to swing my right arm defensively across the front of my body.

'Good night, Jake,' she said. She raised

her left hand to my face and gently drew
her fingertips down my right cheek.

Down her left cheek, across the creases
of her smile, travelled a single large tear.
As we turned away from each other we
did not know that we would touch only
once more.

20

Perspiring, I propelled the boat through the shadow of the bridge. Frimmer was waiting for me some fifty yards further upstream. Back across the fields, under trees, I could see the dark shape of his car shimmering in the rising heat. I steered for the bank. Like a disgruntled hippo Frimmer edged into the reeds. I pulled lightly on my right oar and the prow nearly castrated him. He half-fell, half-climbed aboard and worked his way along to the seat facing me. Once seated he no longer appeared comical.

We sat silent for a time staring across the sunlit meadows toward Browcaister. Church bells were ringing.

'She didn't come back,' I said.

'Stop shouting!' he ordered, exasperated. 'I had enough of that over the telephone yesterday.'

'Sorry, sir.'

'Take us out to midstream.'

'Right.' We drifted gently in the perfect day. Frimmer trailed a hand in the water.

'So,' he said. 'Our Madelaine assaulted you. Miss Sykes saw it and ran tittle-tattling to Mrs Gridley. Mrs Gridley had words with Madelaine, presumably on the lines of 'my house is a respectable house' and Madelaine swep' out.'

'That's probably it. But — '

'Hang on, Bull. Are you in trouble with Mrs Gridley?'

'Not really. She's a bit offish, but I think she's settled on the version: 'poor accident-shocked foreign gentleman unexpectedly assaulted by cheap English girl who's no better than she should be.' '

'But you and Mrs Gridley are still on speaking terms?'

'Well — yes. Bit frosty yesterday but civil.' I paused, sculled the boat lightly against the current. 'This morning I got an extra sausage for Sunday breakfast — one more than Albert.'

'Promising,' said Frimmer. I was not sure what he meant. I watched a pair of sharp-arsed ducks dipping for their breakfast. 'This is what you'll do,' said Frimmer.

'Yes, sir?'

'You persuade Mrs Gridley not to relet that room. If necessary offer to redecorate it for her. Try anything you like but keep that room empty.'

'But Madelaine won't come back. She's taken every — '

'Christ!' groaned Frimmer, banging his fist on the side of the boat. 'Will you stop your yattering and do some listening? Perhaps even some thinking!'

'Sir.'

'Did you seriously believe that she would try and kill you in that house while she was still living there?'

'Well, I suppose — '

'Suppose is shit, Bull! In every case we've reopened she's never been seen anywhere close to the victim at time of death. Surely you realised you were safe while she was close? While she was with you, you were only at risk on the streets. Now you're at risk everywhere. Got it?'

'But what about her room?'

'You don't think she left without having

a set of keys cut, do you? I'm sure your landlandy has a spare set — probably leaves 'em hanging on a hook in her kitchen.'

'She does. I see what you mean.'

'Good. I do prefer my detective sergeants bright rather than bewildered. I would also prefer not to be struck by that low branch.' He allowed himself a moment to enjoy sarcasm, and for me to wrestle with the oars. 'Madelaine arrived at West House very late last night. It seems she's settling in there rather than in her flat?'

'Will you put D.I. Green back in there?'

'Whaddya mean, will I? I moved her back in as soon as I heard your two tarts had been killed. Some of us keep up with the play.'

I concentrated on pulling us clear of a crowded launch. We watched it go past, rocked on its wake.

'Now, Bull, as soon as she leaves West House, Madelaine I mean, we'll contact you by radio. So you now work on a one hour radio check. If you hear from us that she's on the loose you will immediately switch to continuous transmission/reception. Got that?'

'Yes, sir.'

'We'll then be able to monitor you very closely. In addition, I'm issuing you a firearm.' He looked up and down the river, then, to my astonishment, put his hand in his jacket pocket and produced a pistol in a shoulder-holster. 'Here.' He passed the bundle to me below gunwale level. I took it, put it under my coat on the seat. 'And sign.' From another side pocket he produced pad and pen. There was something ludicrous about these actions. And frightening. I'm not sure what expression crossed my face as I wrote my name.

'All right,' he said, sharply. 'So maybe I'm alarmist. But you know well enough why we've not tailed, filmed or bugged her. We *have* to get this right without the risk of her realising we're onto her. So I'm determined you have at least this protection.'

Yes, I thought. The gun is protection for you if she kills me and the inquiry asks if you left me unprotected.

'S.I.U. have five other cases at the moment,' said Frimmer, possibly mind-reading. 'Just take note of the fact *your* case is getting my personal attention. One other thing: you can help yourself by checking out every possible circumstance where a domestic accident might be arranged.'

'I've been doing that every day and — '

'Now do it as if every day was your last.' He stared at me. 'You do realise where you are in all this?'

I nodded, fiddled with an oar.

'How does Mrs Gridley lock up at night?'

'Front door — she only bothers with the mortise, usually forgets about the bolt. The back door's a simple key lock, but there are two bolts. She locks all three.'

'Right. You fix that front mortise as soon as you can. Make it easy for our Miss Grey to get in. Not the sort of thing Mrs Gridley's likely to check, is it?'

'No, sir. Like most other people — if the catch clicks she'll assume it's locked.'

'Good. But make sure the lock on your

door still works.'

'Yes, sir.' I decided not to tell him about the wedge.

'Now take me back to the bank.'

In stepping from the boat he managed to put one foot in the water. On dry land he turned to look into my absolutely straight face. The last word was his.

'Get this boat back to the hiring point. Then keep away from water until we've got her. No boats, no swimming, no evening riverside strolls with Mrs G. or Evelyn.'

'Sir.'

Without wishing me luck he turned away and set off across the field toward his car. I half-hoped for a bull of a different sort, but the field was Frimmer's in several senses.

Mrs Gridley was delighted by the suggestion I might redecorate the empty room for her. Her enthusiasm depressed me. If she was willing to forgo rent and also pay out for paint and paper it was clear how she construed the events of the last two days. The hearsay about Italian morality had been totally dispelled by my

225

upright and gentlemanly conduct during a period of adversity. My refusal to succumb to the advances of 'that woman who used to live here' had branded me a gent in Mrs Gridley's eyes. Just how deeply I was threatened by her romantic dreams was confirmed when I suggested taking Tuesday afternoon from work to start on the room. To my dismay she quite seriously contemplated missing her Bingo session to stay with me. Greater love — . With some difficulty I dissuaded her.

By the Tuesday lunchtime Mrs Gridley had stripped Madelaine's room of its soft furnishings and smaller pieces of furniture. I came home from the library and found her piling the rolls of wallpaper and cans of paint in the centre of the room. Our voices echoed hollowly against the bare boards and windows. She went downstairs while I went to my room, checked my radio, changed into my oldest clothes. Then she came back upstairs with a pot of coffee and a large plate of ham sandwiches. While I threw her dust-cloths over the dressing-table and the bed, she poured me coffee, rearranged the sand-wiches and got deep into her mother hen rôle. I wanted her out of the way but could not risk antagonising her. However, as soon as I mentioned the word 'Bingo' she looked at her watch, said she had to get ready and go. Fifteen minutes later I heard her call goodbye and the front door slammed. I was alone. I continued working. I planned to complete most of the stripping and preparation that after-noon; a programme that related to my other aim: to check the whole room for any clue that might tell me how I was to die.

About half an hour before Mrs Gridley was due back I stopped work. There was no evidence anywhere in that room as to how Madelaine meant to kill me. Nothing had been concealed in the wardrobe or dressing-table; the stitching of the mate-rial on the bed base was undisturbed; the mattress was unmarked. Nor did I find any sign of interference with the floor-boards or wainscoting. None of the electrical fittings had been tampered with; there were no loose or exposed wires that might easily be linked to an electrical appliance such as a faulty electric fire.

Relieved and disappointed, I went into my room, checked the radio, collected a screwdriver and a pair of pliers. This was the opportunity for me to adjust the lock on the front door. I stood at the bottom of the stairs and listened. The house was quiet. I tested the door-catch and the lock. Someone else had beaten me to it. The deadlock mechanism made the right noise but did not engage. At any time of the day or night anyone with a key could get in. I shut the front door.

I walked up the stairs, went back to my room, put the unused screwdriver and pliers away in the same drawer where I kept my door wedge. Then I checked the lock on my own door. It worked perfectly. I listened to my breathing, looked out of the window at a large cloud passing between me and the sun. I felt cold. For the first time I had something to say when that radio light came on again.

21

My radio and I (say that in a royal plummy voice) developed a relationship which, I suspect, characterises a nagging marriage. The red light was always reminding, reproaching, and in its spiteful glare I became increasingly sullen. Worse still, the radio offered nothing: no reports of movements, no suggestions that waiting might soon be over. Psychologists have discovered that red light stimulates the brain and pituitary gland. From this is deduced the theory that sexual activity is also stimulated. Ha! My little red lamp could not compete with the deflations of facing Evelyn Sykes and Mrs Gridley at breakfast.

And there was no Una and Kathy any more; no love triangle. I seemed to be carrying a ridiculous amount of grief for a couple of tarts. The longer I waited for Madelaine the more I wondered if my grief was for someone else. With only an emasculated door lock to watch there was plenty of time for wondering.

Inevitably, I drew closer to Albert. There were absurd parallels in our situations; loneliness was simply the most obvious. Several evenings when I was not completing the redecoration of Madelaine's room, Albert and I went drinking together. Usually, we came back with him more fuddled than me — but not always. I was fraying a bit at the edges; not only through drinking but also in declining physical fitness. And external signs were clear: Evelyn's disapproving stare at breakfast time; Mrs Gridley's prim-pursed mouth, her banging down of plates and cutlery. My watchful colleagues also disapproved, and my one-eyed, red-eyed 'wife' had something to say.

Frimmer sounded far more menacing on the radio than along the length of a rowing boat. My first reaction to his anger was acceptance of it. I *was* a stupid bastard, was jeopardising everything, and, yes, he could have my guts for garters. But he made one mistake:

he nagged for too long.

Hastily, I adjusted the volume control. There was no one else in the house that afternoon, but neighbours were within bellowing distance. I sat back and waited for Frimmer to shut up. By the time I was allowed to speak again I was decently rehearsed.

'In the last two months I've been continuously on duty twenty-four hours a day without a single break.' He started to roar but I cut him short. 'Sorry, sir. Not only am I continuing to have some sort of social life because I *need* it but also because it would look odd to Madelaine or anyone else if I began to live like a monk. I will continue to go out with Albert.'

He spluttered a bit, but I knew I had a victory: cheap, shoddy and silly, but a victory.

I celebrated that evening with Albert. The only damper was being caught in a thunderstorm between the pub and The Larches. I left Albert in the hall talking to the newel-post and rushed upstairs to change my clothes and have a bath. It was also time to check my hair again.

Locked in the bathroom I examined my hair in the mirror. That deep Italian blackness appeared to have faded slightly. As I unpacked the hair-dye kit I giggled a trifle girlishly at the pun: her name was Grey. I regarded myself sternly in the mirror. Better choose ageing rather than insanity. Was that a matter of choice? I rinsed my hair, applied the dye, stayed crouched over the sink while it seeped into every strand. To help it spread, and also to relax my neck, I turned my head very slowly from side to side.

How ironic that my life was saved not by the combined talents of S.I.U., nor by my own skills, but by the requirements of the cosmetic industry. Had it not been necessary to crouch over the sink I might never have spotted the minute scratch marks round a screw in the side panel of the bath.

My legs wanted to take me to the bath, my hands gripped the sink to prevent me spraying dye all over the room. Just before the world ended I was able to move. Having inspected the bath panel: black-painted hardboard held in place by ornamental brass screws, I tiptoed to my room, grabbed some tools and got back to the bathroom before anyone else tried to use it.

Carefully, I removed the side panel. Light fell across the legs of the bath so that they appeared to tuck themselves coyly under the cast-iron belly. No elderly fluff rested on them. Such cleanliness! Had my hair not been so damp it would have risen on the back of my neck. But I could see nothing wrong. Disappointment biting, I lay down and began to wriggle as far under the bath as possible. I didn't get far; the belly of the bath hung low over the floor-boards. But Madelaine was slimmer and smaller than me. I pushed my arms under the bath and began feeling my way along its far flank.

My right hand touched a wire. Even as I snatched my hand away my mind was registering that it must be safe. Cautiously, I explored further. A wire, similar to that in a lead on an electric fire, was attached to each back leg of the bath and led down to and under the floorboards. The wires were sheathed except where they looped round the metal legs of the bath. The way in which they were fixed suggested the wires might easily be dragged clear. I left them in position.

I crawled out from under the bath, sat with my back against the wall. What was it like to be electrocuted? It might feel much the same as a fatal heart attack. That was it. Madelaine was onto another winner. An ex-convict, believed to be in poor health, dies of a heart attack in a bath. But. The 'but' was that the corpse, my corpse, might show signs inconsistent with a heart attack. So how did we explain electrocution? I stood up, walked round the room.

The bathroom, like my bedroom next door, had been converted from an old attic room. It was modern conversion and no one had made the mistake of fitting any ordinary electric plug sockets. So it had to be the heated towel-rail: standard type, oil-filled, electrically heated. Before I could inspect it Albert pounded on the door. I bellowed at him, said I was nearly finished. The bath panel was replaced in seconds. I collected my gear, wrapped the hair-dye kit and tools in my towel, checked I'd flushed the stained cotton wool I had used down the lavatory. I got into my room and locked the door before Albert returned. I sat on the bed and thought about being electrocuted to death.

The wiring to the towel-rail could be tampered with just enough to suggest to an investigator it might become unsafe. And it was conveniently sited close to the end of the bath. If someone really stretched for a towel they could reach with a wet hand and — . The slippery wet body would slide back into the bath and, if not already dead, might well drown. Such possibilities refreshed my mind about some of the files I had read earlier in the year: electrocutions, heart attacks, drownings.

Now for the main problem: how to get electricity to the wires attached to the bath? That would be the real cause of my death. Where did the wires go to? Having just decorated Madelaine's room I knew there was nothing there. In any case her room was at the far end of the landing, beyond mine, beyond Mrs Gridley's. Not even Madelaine could have taken up all those floor-boards without anyone else noticing. In any case it would be unlikely she would be able to whip out so long a length of wire immediately after I died. Not even if greased? No. And the idea didn't fit somehow.

I began to smile at the thought that what that arrangement lacked was elegance of execution. It wasn't clever enough, refined enough for Madelaine; especially when judged against her past record of successes. Still smiling, I looked thoughtfully toward the bathroom as if hoping X-ray vision would take me through the wall that separated the bathroom from my room.

Then I laughed out loud. Madelaine was just as clever, skilful, and elegant as I had come to believe. Still chuckling, I got off the bed and then, very carefully, dragged it away from the wall.

22

'Risky,' said Jim, scratching his nose. 'Too risky?'

'Not if you're Madelaine Grey,' I said, looking at him sideways from my end of the bench. We were back in that garden, and no drunks dozed in the shade, probably because there was a uniformed man posted in the alleyway.

'Hmm. And if you've got away with several other killings — '

'Right, Jim. When you think of some of the things she's set up then this plan for killing me is simple. There was far more risk involved getting into a public park in a wet suit, swimming in unknown waters in the night.'

'Yes,' said Jim. 'And she was prepared to risk a fight to the death with Abercrombie if her surprise attack didn't succeed; a fight with a man perhaps stronger than she. So she took on all the risks of him yelling for help, of being

237

discovered, of starting police inquiries, and even — even of dying in the attempt.'

'Maybe that last possibility didn't bother her much. Dying for the cause might fit pretty well with her particular madness.'

'And now she's murdered two tarts in broad daylight.'

'So we believe,' I said.

Jim looked away from me. In the silence we both looked up at Browcaister roofs drying out after yet another midday thunderstorm.

'So, you reckon she sees you as easy meat?' said Jim, at last.

'Yes. She has me on known territory and has access. She can get into the house whenever we're all out and lock herself away in her old room. Risky but not difficult. She can deadlock the door of her room from inside so if Mrs Gridley tried to get in she'd think the lock was broken. She'd have to wait until next day to get a locksmith by which time I'm dead and Madelaine's gone. But, in fact, there's no reason why Mrs Gridley or anyone else would want to get into that room.'

'I think she's more likely to move in at night,' said Jim.

'Yes. Either relatively early when Evelyn's retired, Albert and I are out drinking, and Mrs Gridley's bingo-ing, or much later when I'm the only one up and preparing for my late bath.'

'Late as in deceased?'

I looked at him.

'Er — sorry,' said Jim.

'Madelaine could watch the bathroom window from the back alley, see me pull down the blind, then nip round to the front door and let herself in. Once she's in my bedroom, she fishes out the wires I found taped under the fitted carpet under my bed. When she hears me splashing about in the bath next door she connects the wires with the wall socket.'

'That's the end of Corelli.'

'So she hopes. Anyway, she pulls the wires clear and takes them with her. She leaves my room, shutting the door behind her, and slips out of the house. My death is attributed to loose wiring in the heated towel-rack.'

'You making it sound easy explains why

you asked for a film crew in a house opposite The Larches.'

'Pictures of her entering and leaving give us another screw to turn.'

'So you're not entirely sold on the effectiveness of using your resurrection to break her down?'

'No. I understand the uselessness of me rushing out of the bathroom crying 'Aha'. All we get for that is an attempted murder charge. But Frimmer's plan is equally a gamble.'

'You're very sure, Jack.'

'I am now. I'm seeing a lot of things a lot more clearly.'

'Sounds like it. Tell me, what'll you be doing in the bathroom once you know she's in the house?'

'First of all I make a lot of noise running the bath. That tells her I'm in there, it covers any noise she makes getting into my room, and it covers any noise I make taking the side panel off the bath. Then I'll be lying on the floor beside the bath watching the wiring round the cast-iron legs. I've left it connected but moved it down near the floor so I can see it from the other side. When she drags it clear I know I'm supposed to be dead. I give her time to get away and then quietly replace the side panel. Even more quietly I get into the bath.'

'Christ! I don't fancy that. If something goes wrong it might still be — '

'Yes, yes, Jim. Thought of that. I'll see if my plastic duck melts. You know, I did suggest to Frimmer that I detach the wires from the bath and hook 'em up elsewhere. But oh, dear me, no, said Frimmer. Mustn't do anything to raise her suspicions!'

'Then you wait to be discovered?' said Jim, hastily. He didn't want to get involved in that other war.

'I do. I act dead or nearly dead, depending on the wit of whoever breaks the door down. There'll be an emergency phone call about my poor mother so I don't have to lie there all night. Whoever comes to fetch me gets frightened when I don't answer, and rouses the house. That's the theory, anyway.'

'Let's hope it works that way in practice,' said Jim, sombrely.

The church clock struck three; the mellow notes dipping into the rose garden. An English afternoon. Ha! And time for me, yet again, to check my radio.

'This is getting worse than a clocking-on job,' said Jim, as I took the radio out of my pocket.

The red light was on. I pressed the button. The light stayed on. I pressed the button again. The light leered at me. On the point of shaking the thing, I realised Jim was staring at me with *that* expression on his face. He saw me as a candidate for West House.

'Christ!' I said.

'Maybe it is, Jack. Better answer and find out.'

The Duty Officer was brusque enough, handed me straight on to Frimmer.

'O.K. to talk, Bull?'

'Of course, sir. Only Jim Douglas with me.'

'Thought you ought to know at once that Corelli's dead.'

'How?'

'Not sure yet. Probably heart. We're arranging a post-mortem for tomorrow.'

'Frimmer, you are a butcher!' I said, curtly.

Jim twitched a bit, stared at me, convinced about West House.

'Who the hell — ' began Frimmer.

'Shut up and listen!' I said. 'Since we've got a body we may as well use it. So I want it unmarked. Stop the P.M. Got it?'

'I hear you but — '

'No buts. You want a body in the bath and I don't want it to be mine.' The silence was so long I began to wonder if my insolence had given *him* a heart attack. I had no use for Frimmer's body.

'D'you think we could get away with *that*?' asked Frimmer.

'Yes, sir,' I said, very slightly polite. 'Once Madelaine Grey is clear of the house, and assuming I've survived, we can get Corelli's body in through the bathroom window. Then you can really enjoy yourself. Have a real ambulance, real doctor, even tip off your local editor friend to send a reporter to the scene.'

'But — '

'No buts. It's easy enough to keep him

fresh for a day or two. I'm pretty sure she won't keep us waiting much longer than that.'

'Yes, Bull, but what about the others in the house?'

'Don't wear your biggest boots.'

'Now just —'

'No just anything. Someone's coming.' I switched off.

'Bloody 'ell,' said Jim, half-admiring, half-alarmed. 'You're a liar as well as insubordinate.'

'So? How's he to know anyone's near by? And if you think I'm sitting at the end of a radio link while he bollocks me you can think again.'

'What's with all this incisiveness, Jack?'

'Two months waiting to be murdered, that's what. And the only offers from Frimmer in that time is the blame for those tarts and the loan of a totally useless pistol. Now he's going to find out that the man in the field is the man in charge. I must've seemed a right bloody fool to the rest of you — me meekly going along with all this crap. If Frimmer wants please sir, and thank you sir, then I want

244

one hundred per cent ungrudging coop-eration. Ungrudging and on my terms. 'Sacrificial Bull', he said. I've not forgotten that and I'm not expendable for the glory of S.I.U.'

'Oo, you *are* masterful,' said Jim, mincingly.

There was a moment of silence, then our laughter drifted across the garden.

I got back to Belmont Road just before six o'clock. As I walked toward The Larches I noticed there was an unidenti-fied car parked on the left hand side and about fifty yards from The Larches. I thought I knew who it belonged to but decided to check.

When I got into my room I radioed through to the Duty Officer on the 6 p.m. call. He was expecting to hear from me.

'Thought you'd spot something, Jack,' he said. 'Matter of fact I've won a quid on it.'

'Who from?'

'Be telling,' he said, maliciously. 'Yes, you're right. We've got a room in number forty-two, not quite opposite you. Two men, Dicks and Francis, don't think you know 'em. They'll share round the clock watch. And they're ready to film as soon as you or we give the word. They're on your frequency as Night Owl, so all conversations are now three-way. Got that?'

I assured him I had, welcomed Night Owl. Dicks or Francis curtly acknowledged and then we all switched off. I stayed sitting on my bed staring at the bedside table and the items I had put on it next to the lamp: a small can of grease and a packet of paper tissues. That bathroom window would have to open and close silently. As the grave, I thought, and heard an echo of Jim Douglas's laughter.

23

Madelaine kept me waiting another forty-eight hours. Two days of suspense, of hourly radio checks, of bizarre triangular conversations with the Duty Officer and Night Owl. Worse still: two more nights.

On those two nights I packed my shoulder-bag, draped my towel over it, checked the appearance of my room, walked quietly onto the dark landing, shut but did not lock my door, went into the bathroom, locked myself in. Paused for breath and listened to the sleeping house.

A harder thing to do was to stand at the window pretending not to look out into the dark garden that crouched round the patch of light thrown onto the lawn; a patch darkened in the centre by my shadow. I was a perfect target at the window. As I lowered the blind I was only slightly consoled that my death had to appear accidental.

The hardest thing to do was to get into the bath. How carefully and deliberately, skin spikey with goose pimples, I approached the steaming water; how infinitesimally slowly I tested it with a forefinger — as if my speed of movement could relate to an electric current. And how athletically I sprang dripping from the water when I heard a board creak on the landing! Truth was, that despite our careful planning, I believed Madelaine clever enough to pass like a slim silver shark through all our nets. She might leave West House, get to Browcaister unseen, then break into The Larches by a door or window at the back, thus avoiding Night Owl perched opposite the front door. That she might be caught afterwards — when my colleagues heard me dying on their radios — was no consolation. I meant to be in at another's death.

Thursday evening I came to the house at 5.30 p.m., washed, changed, lay on my bed. At 6 p.m. I switched on my radio.

'No cause for alarm.' It was Frimmer

speaking. 'But she may have given us the slip.'

'Explain.' How could I sound so calm?

'She did not return to West House to join D.I. Green for afternoon tea as had been arranged. And she's not at her flat.'

'So how long's she been running free?'

'Two hours.'

As Kathy must have done I felt an agonising pain shear across my gut. Unlike Kathy, I saw not the demented face of Madelaine but the tall suffocating shape of Frimmer.

'Two hours?'

'Yes, Jack.'

'So she could be in Browcaister by now?'

'Possible,' said Frimmer.

'Right, sir. I'll have a quiet evening drinking with Albert Hammond. I doubt if even the heaviest thunder-storm'll put him off. Drink makes him sleepy once his bladder's emptied, so that'll help. Evelyn Sykes is still on holiday. Mrs G. always sleeps well after bingo and a nightcap. When I get back here I'll wait up and have a late last bath. My body ready?'

'Oh — Corelli: yes. And we're only half an hour away.'

So. He wasn't in his bunker. Perhaps he was in that safe house I'd been taken to. Once again that eerie feeling that he knew just a little more than I did; that even in the hour of my death his deviousness still squatted between us like a poisonous toad.

'Anything else, Bull?'

'Not a thing, sir. Listening. Out.'

Going drinking with Albert took slightly longer than the evolution of man. It felt as painful. At long last we returned to The Larches. It had stopped raining but the muggy heat of the night suggested other thunderstorms lurked at the end of the street. Steadying Albert on the doorstep, I put my key in the lock, opened the front door. There was a movement in the hall. I grabbed at Albert, swung him in front of me.

'Hey!' he said.

'It's all right. I'm holding onto you,' said I, gripping tightly.

'Well!' said Mrs Gridley. Her sigh of

exasperation merged with my sigh of relief.

'Evening, my dear,' said Albert. Then: 'Excuse me!'

He weaved along the hall to the downstairs lavatory. I looked at Mrs Gridley and shrugged with what I hoped was a Mediterranean gesture.

'Man's a fool,' she said, shortly. 'Good job you're a bit more *sensible* about drink.'

'Have you had a good time, Mrs Gridley?'

'Yes. But not my lucky night tonight. Well, I'm for bed. I might say something we all regret if I'm here when Mr Hammond comes out. Goodnight.' She stepped across to the board, flicked the 'In' signs against her name, my name and Albert's. Evelyn's name had been taken down while she was on holiday. That space lay above the one where Madelaine's name had lain. And all the time I was talking with Mrs Gridley perhaps Madelaine was upstairs waiting in her old room. Waiting for me.

'Good night, Mrs Gridley,' I said,

operating the useless catch on the door-lock.

'Good night, dear,' she called, ascending the stairs. She did not turn for a last farewell glance. Then Albert pulled the chain, tottered into the hall while dragging up his zip. I wanted no more of him. I reached the top of the stairs before he reached the bottom.

In my room I snatched up my radio, steadied my breathing. No need to wait for my hands, we weren't using morse. I switched on.

'Bull here. Has she got into the house, Night Owl?'

'Not that we've seen, Sergeant. Just Mrs Gridley, and then you and Hammond returning.'

'No one earlier?'

'No. No one.'

So she wasn't waiting in that locked room. Perhaps she was waiting out in the alley; waiting for me to pull down the bathroom blind.

'Right,' I said. 'I'm now keeping my radio on continuous reception. Anything to report I want it instantly — commentary not history. Got that?'

'Yes, Sergeant,' said Night Owl.

'I think what — hold it!' I stopped talking while Albert blundered past my door. 'O.K., I — '

'What's up?' It was Frimmer. He sounded as if he was in the next room, the bathroom.

'O.K., sir. Just Albert going past the door. Are you still half an hour away from me?'

'No,' he said. 'We're just round the corner.'

'We?'

'Me, some colleagues and your dead body.'

'You're that sure?'

'No, but let's be smart, shall we? She's certainly given us the slip so we'd better assume it's tonight.'

'Yes, sir.'

'It's 10.55 now,' said Frimmer.

'That means I've about twenty minutes to wait before I run my bath. I'll stay listening.'

'And us,' said Frimmer. 'And Night Owl.'

'Sir,' said Dicks or Francis.

'Good luck,' said Frimmer. 'Listening. Out.'

I swung my feet from the floor, stretched out on the bed. Beside me, on the bedside cabinet and next to the bedside lamp, the radio also lay quiet, occasionally emitting a soft hiss or crackle. Behind the curtains heavy droplets of rain struck resoundingly against the glass; the rain Albert and I had dodged. I turned my cheek against the pillow, looked at the radio. Then I began to shake.

24

11.15 p.m. Bath time.

For the last time I packed my shoulder-bag: pistol first then plastic mac, talcum powder, toilet-bag, pliers, screwdriver, radio, rubber gloves. I swung the strap over my left shoulder, then draped strap and bag with a bath-towel. The material of the towel felt warm and rough under my left ear, gave off the familiar furry smell of soap and self and laundering.

I looked round the inhabited room: toothpaste and toothbrush in the glass above the little sink, wardrobe door ajar, the clothes hanging neat in their ranks, papers and open briefcase on the table. Pyjamas, sprawling across the bed, waiting for me. I switched off the bedside lamp, acutely aware of other wires lying under the carpet. Yet I was more than calm, was floating on that feeling of surrender that subverts as one is wheeled from the ambulance into the hospital.

I locked myself in the bathroom. Except for the pistol, I unpacked my bag onto the side table by the sink, then walked to the window. Raising my right hand to the blind-cord I checked that the window catch was off. Traces of grease glinted on the inner edges of the window frames. Will the real Corelli please come in? Lightning flickered, rain prodded at the window. The garden was invisible through the rain-starred glass. But what would I have done if I had seen a movement? Very slowly I lowered the blind. Two minutes was the time needed to walk briskly from the back alley to Belmont Avenue and along to The Larches. I had paced it out several times. I urinated, pulled the chain, walked to the sink, ran the taps over my face-flannel and bath-towel. They took the water greedily. Then I turned off the taps, listened. No sound out on the landing, but to be safe I held the radio close to my mouth.

'Bull here. Come in, Night Owl.'
'Night Owl here, Sergeant.'

'Anything?'

'No. Some people in the street, hurrying. It's raining hard at the moment. We reckon our pictures'll be poor in this weather. The lightning don't help.'

'Do what you can. Listening. Out.'

I walked over to the bath. What to do? Had she got through our nets? If she was already in her old room she would be wondering why I had not yet run the bath. I removed my jacket, my shadow falling across the blind. The radio crackled sympathetically with the storm. As I turned toward it thunder rumbled closer than before. The possibility of being struck by lightning if I survived electrocution by Madelaine was grotesquely appropriate. The red eye of the radio began to blink.

'Bull here.'

'Night Owl. Someone at the gate. A woman in a dark mackintosh, wearing some kind of rain-hat, carrying a large shoulder-bag. She's stopped at the gate.'

'You filming?'

'Yeah, but — . She's coming in! She's

in the porch. Looks like the door's opening.'

'Frimmer here. No more talk until Bull reports. Listening. Out.'

The interjection was so brutal I squeezed the radio as if trying to crush its toughened case. Then I put it down beside the sink. Then I was all right.

I pulled on my gloves, picked up the screwdriver, stepped across to the bath, put the plug in and turned on both taps. I knelt on the floor and started to remove the side panel from the bath. Having greased the screws when I greased the window they came out easily; no need for pliers. As I lifted the hardboard sheet away from the bath, sweat ran into my eyes, yet the panel weighed so little. I lowered it flat on the floor, laid myself on top of it, looked under the bath. The wires were there. To slow myself down, to slow everything down, I counted to ten. Then I reached up, turned off the hot tap, left the cold running, had been advised of the adverse effects of hot water on a stale corpse. Not that it mattered. (All that nonsense of mine about Frimmer using a real ambulance, a real doctor. Only his own man would pretend not to notice the condition of the corpse.) The adverse effects of hot water! Whatever it was going to do a dead body that water was not going to do anything to me. Somewhere close, yards, feet, a wall away, Madelaine was getting ready to kill me.

I stirred the water vigorously with the plastic-handled back-brush. (I had lied to Jim about a plastic duck.) I turned off the cold tap, tossed the brush into the water. No more touching. Silence. I looked under the bath. The wires were still there. I reached back to the sink, gathered up the saturated flannel and bath-towel. The flannel fell into the bath with a satisfactory splash. The towel went in like a tired body.

Kneeling on the floor well clear of the bath, I watched the wires. Waited. The silence felt wrong. I wished I could replicate the farting, slithering sounds a body makes against the bath bottom. Cautiously, I raised my left arm and, with a flick of my forefinger, propelled the pumice stone off the bath edge. The splash and a flurry of rain on the window were simultaneous. I squatted back on my heels, took a deep breath.

One of the wires moved. There was an extraordinary sensation of heat. The soap in the soap dish moved, steamed. There was a bang from the junction box linked to the towel-rail. Then the wires were gone. Madelaine had killed me.

The weight of anticlimax was so enormous I lay down again, rested my head on my folded arms. I tried to control my breathing, slowing it, keeping it shallow. Listened to the silence. Another of our suppositions about Madelaine was correct. Nothing so crude as shoving bare wires directly into a plug socket with the risk of noise, wrong fuses blowing or a flashburn on the underside of the bath. And nothing so vulgar as water sizzling! Lying there I might even have persuaded myself it had not happened. But the wires had gone. The 'correct' fuse had blown. (I had not even identified a wire leading to the towel-rail!)

As though confirming my death, Madelaine trod on that creaking board on the landing. We both froze, only a flimsy door between us; killer and victim waiting for any third person to hear the noise. Eternity. When she moved again the only sound to reach me was the faintest rustle of rainwear against the stair-post. I lay still. When my watch had counted twice as long as was necessary I crawled to the sink, reached for the radio.

'Bull here. Report.'

'Night Owl here. She's out. Thirty seconds ago. Turned left, walked quickly. Waiting to hear from the Chief Super now.'

'Hold on,' said Frimmer. We waited.

'Now,' said Frimmer. 'Just crossed the end of our street. Stand by.' We waited.

'Frimmer again. Douglas reports she's clear of Brampton Road. We move in five minutes. Out.'

Nobody had asked me how I was. Fortunately, I had things to do.

I replaced the side panel on the bath, wiped off the screwheads. Then I dragged the saturated towel to the end of the bath, draped it over the bath edge and across the towel-rail. I replaced the screwdriver and unused pliers in my bag on top of the pistol. My toilet-bag and talcum powder I left on the table. I picked up the plastic mac. It emitted that odd creaking, rustling sound that only plastic can utter. So different to the noise of her raincoat.

What was she thinking now as she strode through the storm, rain rattling against that coat? Were her tears for our closeness or relief at her success? Perhaps her thoughts were already set toward her next victim. And why should I think of the possibility of tears?

I discovered I had repacked the mac into my bag. Perhaps too noisy to wear. Better to get wet. Checked the room for the last time. Looked at my watch. How little time a killing takes. Sat on the bathroom stool and waited. When the five minutes had passed my radio blinked obediently.

'Bull here,' I whispered.

'Frimmer. We're ready to move. Are you?'

'Yes. But where is she?'

'Just reported walking into the railway

station. We're still not tailing but got a man there.'

'So it really is all clear?'

'Of course it is! Stand by!'

I switched off the bathroom light, walked carefully across the black room, released the window blind, let it rise slowly. Then I eased up the lower window on its greased frame and the night fell into the room against my thighs.

'Ready now,' I said, speaking into my radio for the last time. Then I put it in my bag, zipped the bag shut, swung the strap over my shoulder. I stepped back from the window and crouched down so I could see through the lower open section. The white gate in the garden wall was suddenly visible in its movement. Black apparitions passed between it and me. I swallowed hard.

The padded end of a ladder settled against the sill. A broad, gorilla-like man swarmed into the room. He stank of dampened cloth, of perspiration. 'Out you go, son,' he whispered.

I half-slipped, half-fell down the ladder into the gloved grasp of two other large men. By their feet lay a long black box. It had handles at the ends not the sides — a coffin for two bearers.

'Over here,' whispered Frimmer.

For a moment I could not see him, then one of the apple trees moved. I went to him, stood beside him, looked back at the house.

'Good job Corelli's to be found in a bathroom,' said Frimmer, quietly. 'All this rain.'

I did not reply. I was peering through the rain watching his team of apes moving the coffin up the ladder. My coffin. I was glad of the darkness, the rain blurring my eyes.

'Clever idea of yours,' said Frimmer.

'Not mine! D'you think I didn't know how you were manipulating me into it — and that poor sod!' I gestured feebly toward the window. Then I was blind. I could feel I had Frimmer by the throat, was forcing his head back against the tree trunk. 'You think I'm fuckin' stupid, don't you — a right mug? And you've known about Corelli all this time, since before I even joined S.I.U.'

'Yes,' said Frimmer, calmly easing my hands from his throat. He could have tossed me back into that bathroom from where we stood. We were locked together in the rain, our four hands clasped together near his neck. But Frimmer had not dodged the question.

'So tell me,' I demanded.

'Two phone calls to the prison, checking the date of his release.'

'Ah.'

'And the caller was a woman.'

'So you knew even *that*. And you never told me.'

'Didn't follow that our target was a woman, did it?' He pushed my hands down to waist height, his waist height.

'No, but — '

'Come on, Bull. What help would it have been for you to know that? Just look back at yourself over the last eight weeks.'

I let my arms fall to my sides. And, presumably, he expected me to believe Corelli really had died of a heart attack, just as he expected me to go on dreaming it had been my own idea to use the body. I turned away, looked up into the rain at the bathroom window. Two men were coming out backwards manhandling an empty box. When they reached the ground the third man stepped out onto the ladder. He wiped a cloth along the sill, then eased down the blind, shut the window to within inches of the sill. He ducked down low, made a jerking movement with his right hand. The bathroom light came on, a cord ran free, he completed the closing of the window, came down the ladder.

'Let's go,' said Frimmer, softly.

We walked diagonally across the lawn to the gate, arrived at the same time as the other three men. One of them waved us ahead. Frimmer opened the gate, ushered me through into the alley.

'Welcome to the land of the living,' he said.

25

Tuesday afternoon, a warm autumn day. Wearing the dark suit I had worn most often as Corelli, I sat on the back seat of Frimmer's Jaguar while the driver guided the car toward West House. Frimmer sat next to me.

'You hot?' he asked, swaying toward me. He was. His jacket was on the seat between us, his shirt-sleeves were rolled up. A sweaty, hairy toad blinking at me in the strong sunlight. Mr Toad and his big car.

'No, sir. It's cool enough in here.' Soon enough he would discover what I was concealing under my jacket.

'See you got your hair black again. Never suspected you'd be the type to go grey under stress.' Need to talk reflected nervousness. His career might be balanced on the outcome of events about to begin; events I would control. 'You still look the part,' he said, placatingly.

'I need to, sir. I'm your last card,' I said, maliciously.

He gave me a dirty look. I knew I had him by the short and curlies and was enjoying the experience to the full; partly because I knew it was to be a rare experience. I doubted if any other S.I.U. case would be so much a chapter of accidents.

The plan to tail Madelaine had failed. Our man had seen her onto the train, non-stop to Warwick it was, and had radioed ahead for her to be watched from there. No need to risk getting on the train with her. Then she had pulled the emergency handle. It was the last train, nearly empty; no one saw. The next we knew she was back in West House full of a four day holiday way up north. She had even got leaflets from an exhibition that was on in Durham. Probably picked them up on the way *to* Browcaister. Imagine trying to prove that. And, of course, Night Owl's film was not good enough to be evidence because of the effects of the bad weather.

I had also enjoyed thwarting Frimmer's

argument that her careful covering of tracks had anything to do with any suspicion we were on to her. I had pointed out to him that covering her tracks was habitual, part of her way of life. In her mind, covering tracks was probably as much to do with preparing for the next killing as it was to do with the last.

Her talent for covering tracks had also worked for the double murder of Kathy and Una. The Browcaister police had found the burnt-out wreck of a car which had been reported stolen on the day of the killings. The petrol tank must have been full and there had been cans of petrol in the boot. All that Forensic could tell us was that items of plastic and rubber had been incinerated. The only other recognisable object, apart from remnants of petrol cans, was a deeply burned and twisted knife blade. Impossible to tell what it had been used for. Nor had Forensic found any evidence in the ground near the fire. The wreck was in an isolated quarry and had not been found for a month; a month of many thunderstorms.

The only thing that had gone well in Browcaister had been the discovery of my body. The phone call about 'mother' had persuaded Mrs Gridley to tell Albert to break down the door. When the ambulance arrived, with Jim Douglas as a crew member, Mrs Gridley was hysterical. At one point she had sobbed that she had hardly recognised me. She was reassured by Jim who told her that drowned people look different underwater, but she was riled by Albert who told her it was because she had not seen me naked before. The local editor had responded with a discreet report and a photo of me, only to discover that the promised scoop was off. The very last I heard of Mrs Gridley was that she had taken in two men lodgers, one of them a local policeman. Echoes of things past!

Three weeks later a decomposing body was found a hundred miles away in a fenland drain. The evidence indicated that the corpse of Jake Corelli had been there several days and that cause of death was a heart attack. Who or what had induced the attack was not ascertainable.

Apart from Mrs Gridley, Corelli and myself the only other person I felt sorry for was Mr Stone. His frustration must have been awful. It was he who had stumbled on some tantalising evidence in Madelaine's London flat. He discovered she kept record cards of all the manuscripts she had read for her publishers. She read mainly thrillers and kept summaries of plots and main characters. Twenty-four of the cards could not be matched against the list of manuscripts the publishers had sent her. Unfortunately, the D.D.P. said it wouldn't stand up. One problem was that it was very difficult sorting out her cryptic notes in the first place, partly because her employers were rather vague about which manuscripts she had been given. It was not always organised with covering letters etc. More a case of: 'Can you cast your eye over this one as well, dear?' To make matters worse one of the directors pointed out that some of the cards reminded him of thrillers published by other houses. Because there are relatively few ways of killing a man those ways get used over and over again in different books. It had been only too clear what a good defence lawyer would make of that.

'You know D.I. Green's been doing her damnedest inside West House?' said Frimmer, interrupting my recollections.

'But no joy there — either, sir?'

'No. Nothing that's evidence. She reports that Grey has been very moody, although she livened up when she saw Green's copy of the Browcaister paper with the report of your death.'

'At least those details worked out,' I said.

Frimmer turned on me a look of absolute loathing. Fortunately, he had no time to reply.

The driver lowered the glass partition. 'Shall I drive straight in, sir?'

'Yes,' hissed Frimmer.

The great gates to West House were wide open. As we swung into the drive, Arthur watched us from the doorway of his lodge. He had his instructions. In the sunlit hall behind him stood other men;

one was speaking into the telephone. Nobody waved.

The driver slowed the car, but the trees lining the avenue seemed to flick past like eyelashes blinking; unlike last time when I had trudged in the wake of Mrs Athelsteyn-Crump. She was one person I would not meet today. Mr Johnson I would: somehow he was important. I looked up the slope at the allotments. The only obvious change was that the little regiment of cabbages had gone. Mr Johnson.

'Slowly, driver,' said Frimmer. 'Not too much racket when we turn on the gravel. Park over there at the side of the house.'

The car stopped. The faint vibration from the engine ceased. We sat immobile for a long moment while the warmth of the autumn afternoon began to edge into the car. Frimmer looked at his watch.

'3.28. Green's expecting you at 3.30. You have to get this right,' he said.

'Sir,' I said, my hand on the door-handle.

'Watch yourself. She might try again.'

'She won't,' I said, fiercely, and pushed the door shut in his face. The driver coughed into his hand. I wondered which of the three of us was most surprised by Frimmer's expression of concern.

26

I walked past the side of the house, then round the corner to the front door. The shoulder holster felt heavy under my jacket as I raised my hand to the bell. A blonde, desiccated, hard-faced police-woman, disguised as a domestic, opened the door.

'Come in, sir — er — Sergeant. You're expected.' Behind the angular face seethed excitement. She disgusted me. 'You know the way, Sergeant?'

'What? Of course. Anything come up on the monitors?'

'That's our temporary radio room if you want to check.' She pointed at a doorway at the far end of the hall beyond the foot of the stairs.

'No time now,' I said.

True, but also I did not want to face colleagues who would overhear every word spoken in Madelaine's room. I walked to the stairs, passing the row of chairs, the mirror facing them. The banister rail slipped easily through my curved left hand. The stairs drifted downward under my feet. The first floor landing was deserted. Everyone was out walking in the sunshine or hiding from the tension they must surely feel through the floors and walls. I did not look into the first floor mirror but turned immediately toward Madelaine's room. I have no memory of walking along that corridor. I think I did not knock before going in.

They sat facing each other: Madelaine Grey with her back to the windows, Susan Green between her and the bedroom door. Evidently they had been aguing, yet my first impression was also of a pairing, a sense of unity into which I was grossly intruding. It was to do with more than the fact they were both dressed in white. The round blonde head and the slightly elongated brown head pivoted toward me on their graceful neck stems.

I shut the door and leaned against it. Madelaine spoke the name by which she really knew me. I nodded.

'But you — ' she said. She gestured

toward the month-old newspaper lying on the carpet beside Susie's chair. She paused. '*And* you've been upsetting me again, Susie.' Another pause. 'Ah, now I see. You and he are together.' She looked back at me.

Had she cried out, tried to leave, done any violent thing, I could have borne it. But, unerringly, she chose to do the one thing I could not bear. She tucked her legs under her in the chair, then raised right hand to white face and slowly, heartbreakingly, put her thumb in her mouth.

I fell into the nearest chair. She turned her head slightly to one side so she could watch me. Susie sat quite still, her hands grasping the chair arms, knuckles as white as Madelaine's face.

'Who?' whispered Madelaine past her thumb.

'Corelli,' I said, almost as indistinctly, through my aching throat.

'Who was in the bath?'

'I was.'

Her unbalanced mind became possessed by the fact of my resurrection. I doubt if the self-betrayal in her question ever occurred to her. Suddenly, her fear was in the room like a beast. She began to shake. There was a disgusting, cloying smell of warm urine. I looked at Susie who slowly moved her head from side to side. I wondered if the message was that we should say nothing. Eventually, Madelaine looked again at Susie.

'And you?' she said.

'Don't talk to me,' said Susie. 'Talk to the dead man!'

'What can you do for me if you're dead?'

'I can still listen while you talk,' I said.

She raised her left hand, seemed deliberately to disarrange the shining brown crown of her hair. Hair fell across one side of her face as she brought her left arm up against her head, cradling her head in the crook of her elbow. Her eyes widened, glittered; her breathing hissed, her tousled hair began to writhe; drops of venom appeared on her forehead, her contorted cheeks. I did not hear her words, only the hissing; did not see her face, only the Gorgon. Much later, when the rage left her, the drops of venom remained: sweat standing on her forehead, tears from her eyes. Eventually, she folded her hands in her lap.

'Do you miss those two?' she asked in a completely normal voice.

'Who?' I was still stumbling in her madness.

'The two women I killed.'

'You killed them?' said Susie, breathlessly.

'Of course. Isn't that what all this is about?'

As I will never forget her sucking her thumb so I will never forget the sheer physical weight of the irony in that question. 'After all I've suffered I was not going to stand by and watch those women feeding the cancer that had already destroyed my life: sex at any price.'

'And you admit that you murdered them?' asked Susie.

'Silly woman. That's your choice of words. I did what I had to do.'

Aghast, we looked at Madelaine. Somehow, even now, she was eluding us.

'And the men you killed?' I asked.

'What men, Mr Corelli? You seem confused.' The statement was made without guile of any kind.

Knowing it was useless, I recited a list of names. She shook her head at each one of them. We both turned to Susie for help. Madelaine spoke to her first.

'*You* will have to help me.'

'Yes,' said Susie.

'When I got home from the trial, you know — I told you — the trial of the man who raped me, my parents had gone.'

'Gone?' said Susie.

'Yes. While I was in hospital, in a home, and then in court, they sold up the house, everything, without telling me. On the last day of the trial they moved out, left no address. Abandoned me when I most needed them. I came home from that awful courtroom to find my own home full of strangers. Can you imagine what that was like? You won't abandon me now?'

'No,' said Susie, sadly. A long silence.

And now, so belatedly, I understood the real motive. She had done what she had done not because the defence lawyer who smeared her was wrong but because he was right. That was why her parents had abandoned her. They had *known* the lawyer was right. I saw her for what she really was even though I could not find the right words for it. She was some sort of nymphomaniac but motivated also by a second mania (in the literal sense): a mania for self-justification. That fitted with my colleagues' longstanding opinion she was mad. As long as I had clung to the revenge motive I had fed my tenuous belief that she might possibly be sane. Now I knew her.

'Shouldn't we go now?' asked Madelaine.

So we went. What else to do? I led the way. Madelaine, in her stinking dress, followed; Susie behind her.

At the foot of the stairs I stepped forward into the hall. At the same moment Mr Johnson emerged from a side room. Madelaine shouted at him in a high voice, something about saving her from being taken away. As he pulled that vicious gardening knife from his pocket I turned, flipped my jacket button, drew my pistol.

Madelaine stood poised on the bottom step, waiting. Behind her, Susie cried out: 'No, Jack!'

As Mr Johnson stepped forward I took aim and fired one shot into Madelaine's breast.

She fell back into Susie's arms. Mr Johnson's knife clattered to the floor as he put his hands over his face. I knelt on the stairs beside Madelaine, the sleeve of Corelli's dark suit brushed into the blood staining her white dress. I placed the back of my left hand gently against her left cheek. In her dying eyes I saw the recognition of who touched her, who saved her. It was our one moment of total identification. They will never take that moment away from us. Whatever they do.

Behind me the yellow-faced police-woman was trying to drag Mr Johnson from the hall. Frimmer, shouting something from the door of the radio room, came striding forward. Susie sat back on the stairs holding the weight of Madelaine's head on her lap. There appeared to be enough people to cope. I went out into the sunlight.

Very slowly, I walked along the drive, alternately in sunlight and shadow as I passed the great trees. I was almost halfway to the lodge by the time the black car drew up beside me. Frimmer opened the back door, stretched out his hand.

'You aimed at Johnson, didn't you, Bull? He's important to you that way; help you keep your job. I'll take the pistol now.'

I was surprised to find I was still carrying it in my hand. I gave it to him. Then I leaned onto the roof of the car. Frimmer had known full well I still had the gun. What I had believed was an act of my free will was merely another of his manipulations. If he could not have a proof he would have a death. I felt as if his great car had not stopped but smashed into me, crushing me against the trunk of one of the trees.

When I could move I brushed a brown leaf off the roof, then climbed into the car, shut the door. As I did so my sleeve left a broad smear of her blood across the window. Frimmer was talking to me but I heard nothing until, as we approached the lodge at the end of the drive, an ambulance swung in from the lane and the siren was sounded against us.

THE END

Other titles in the
Linford Mystery Library:

DEATH CALLED AT NIGHT

R. A. Bennett

Jimmy Ellis believes his parents have died in a car crash when as a young boy he is taken to live with relatives in Australia. The years pass happily, then the nightmare comes. Terrifying images flit through his mind in the dark — all through the eyes of a child, a witness to grisly events seventeen years before. He begins to delve into the past, and soon he finds himself on the trail of a double murderer — a murderer who is prepared to kill again.